# Veritas' Ark

*A Storm of Wind and Rain Novella*

Jo Seysener

**Veritas** *n. latin*  -   truth

In Roman mythology, Veritas was the goddess of truth, daughter of Chronos, and mother of Virtus. She was also considered a daughter of Zeus, or a creation of Prometheus. She is depicted robed in white, holding a hand mirror.

Veritas is known as the motto of Harvard University and the Dominican Order of the Roman Catholic Church.

# CHAPTER ONE

Behaving as an adult wasn't my strong suit, having grown up without any around me. That didn't excuse me from being sentenced as one.

Pews lined the immense Hall, empty except for a few heartless souls, and me. I waited for my verdict on a cold bench. Hard wood bit into the backs of my shaking legs, shoes tapping nervously on the marble of the dais. I pressed my knees together as fear coursed through me. I broke out into a chilled sweat, despite the airless interior.

I was glad the Hall was devoid of onlookers. If a crowd had been called to watch my Bidding, it would have meant my sentence would be harsh.

The Keepers—in their white robes—murmured quietly beside an ancient tapestry depicting a man pinned to a wooden structure. The plaque below declared him as *The Man on the Tree*. I knew the legend, but nowadays, when someone was hung up on a tree, it meant humans weren't the ones who did it.

I strained to hear the Keepers, wishing I had said more in my defence. My shoes clattered on the floor, echoing. The Keepers fell silent, turning to face me as one. Their faces were blank, unreadable. At a nod, one broke away from the group. I began to rise, but my knees wobbled, and I subsided back onto the bench, pressing the white skirt of my dress smooth with dirty hands, leaving marks.

A false smile fixed itself to my face, anticipating the worst. He was a squat little man, grey and balding. I was glad I had stayed seated—I would have towered over him, and short men with big egos never liked that. The Keeper began to speak but snapped his mouth shut. The grind of his teeth was audible, setting my frayed nerves further on edge. He shook his head, giving me a condescending glare.

"Veritas. You are here far too often. Others we might penalise once, twice—*in a lifetime*—and you...this is your final chance, young woman. Family or no–,"

My stomach clenched at the mention of my parents, and I lost the thread of the Keeper's spiel. His words triggered the smell of my mother's hair, sweet and woodsy, the earthy scent of my father, so like the greenhouse I toiled in every day. It had been so many years since they died, and the memory faded far too quickly.

The Keeper was still rambling. I refocused, trying to catch the thread of his words, but they were the same as always. Responsibility, community awareness, don't anger the Earth...I'd heard it a thousand times, from many different voices. Sighing, I wiggled numb toes inside my boots, hoping he would get to my sentence quickly.

"...and you Create with no regard for what might happen to the rest of us! Your actions are against our laws, which are in place for good reason. While we allow everyone to use their...talents in their work, you go too far. Do you want to anger Her? Creating on a scale like this...you," he spoke in a low voice, shaking a stumpy finger in my face, "should be Outcast."

I cringed inside, hoping my thoughts didn't show on my face. Outcast had been thrown at me a few times, and unless I did something *really* stupid, it wasn't likely they would ever follow through. I hoped. Talking about my ability to Create like it was something evil and rotten like it wasn't the only thing that came naturally to me nearly broke me, though I should have been used to it by now. Without my Creations, I was no one really.

I nodded to show I understood, hoping he wasn't about to toss me out of the community forever for growing a plant with animated tendrils that curled reflexively. Handy for hanging things on, actually. Jase had loved it. It made the intricate work he did twinning the vines so much easier.

But the Keepers didn't see it that way. I was just a hazard they couldn't control. Beady eyes stared into mine, and I realised I was expected to respond.

"I'm sorry?" I offered, attempting to resurrect a smile. His withering gaze told me I'd failed—again.

The Keeper flapped at my half-hearted attempt of an apology, tangling squat arms in his oversized robes. I snorted, covering it with a hacking cough. He extracted his hands, patting at the swath of cloth as he attempted to lord over me, failing magnificently.

"Veritas Tempesta, you are sentenced to collect glass tubes. *Two* baskets," he added when I groaned.

It sounded like an easy job, just two baskets. But I'd have to venture into the ravine—creepy, dark, and overworked. I'd be lucky if there were enough glass left to fill both baskets. The coast, hit hardest when the Last Storm raged, was too far. So, ravine it was. It was an odd place; the ancient bones of lightening scattered about, glassy tubes we melded to contain the few bees left. Still, it could have been a worse sentence.

"Alright," I mumbled. The Keeper's hand landed on my shoulder, and I jerked away, skin crawling.

"Take heed, child. If we summon you to another Bidding, you will find yourself in the Vault."

I stared at him, horrified as tears pricked my eyes. This threat wasn't the same as his repeated attempts to blackmail me into submission; this time, he really meant it. The Keeper nodded, appeased his message had gotten through, dismissing me with a wave. My feet carried me off the dais and halfway to the entry before I knew where I was.

I slipped between the buttress roots of the giant fig that constituted a door to the ancient building and out into the fresh air, glad to be free of the confines of the Hall and its occupants.

I tipped my head back as I left the Hall, staring into the frozen skyscape. Rainbows flitted about, caged in ice that covered our sky. They bounced cheerfully within their confines, showering me in bright, clean light. We lived in the perfect Utopia. I snorted—an unladylike and graceless sound.

Perfect through destruction, that is. It had taken the earth hundreds of years to recover from the Last Storm. Then came the Cleaners, and humanity had changed. There were tales of people being hunted by a cult in the days after the Earth's attacks ceased. No reason was given in our legends, only that they always wore white. No-one living knew what it would be like to have water fall from the sky.

I'd lost a solid hour of work during my Bidding. The Keepers just had to put their foot down about something I did, even if it was useful—and the job they had given me, after all. I shook my head, dirt scattering the shoulders of my white dress—a most impractical colour for a Petrichorist. I snorted again. Fancy name for a gardener, really. Or a botanist? I'd heard that term before but never had that chance to learn more. How could I? All our books were locked away, hidden behind rows of ice.

Happiest with my hands sunk deep in the earth, I gave new life to the stunted plants the Keeper's provided, making tiny changes that tweaked their nature. But not too many changes—which was why I was always in trouble. Dirt scattered my dress, leaving it greyer than white. Why they made us wear white to our Biddings, I would never understand. It wasn't as though we were ever innocent; the Keepers manipulated their own rules too much for that. I shuddered at the thought of being dragged back into the Hall any time soon. Every moment in that empty space confined me.

I spread my arms, letting the fresh air kiss my skin beneath the rainbow light. Nothing should be caged in. Nothing.

Including me.

Thanks to their Laws, I wasn't free. Not free to Create, not free to read the books in the Library. Its white arches had been carved by one of the eruptions that speared minerals through the soil like glistening swords in the frozen light when the Earth had fought back. Too many years of us pilfering her minerals, of carving Her open. When the Last Storm broke, She had awoken, jarred from Her slumber by lightning that ravaged the surface.

Footsteps thumped the ground behind me. I knew he had followed me from the Hall, which made me feel a little better, knowing I'd had company. A quick glance over my shoulder assured me I was correct. Swinging long arms and stuffing a roll in his mouth was Jase—named after some far-distant relative and a myth that had something to do with cats, which no longer existed; nothing larger than an insect survived, apart from humans. There was a picture of a cat in a stained-glass window in the Library, though. Legend had it; they were little clawed monsters who dug up your garden and ate flying lizards. During the day, the window sat dull, the cat's gaze fixed, staring. At night when the rainbows became auroras, its eyes glowed green, seeming to follow me whenever I passed beneath its otherworldly gaze. I hated it.

Briefly wondering what it looked like from

inside the Library, I guessed it wouldn't matter. If I *ever* were allowed inside, I certainly wouldn't be looking at windows. Rumour said there were rows of tomes that detailed family history, going back to the source—to the Last Storm. The thoughts of turning pages in a real book, learning something—anything—about our past, our families, was a burning need inside me I had tried to quell for years. But it was a dream; unless you were the Librarian, you never got to go inside.

Jase coughed to get my attention.

"Hey V, why don't you Create a tree that grows these? Cooking them takes forever." He waggled the roll at me in emphasis.

I shrugged, knowing it would irritate him, and was rewarded with a crease across his brow, which turned into a smile.

"Just broaden your talents, whip out something the world hasn't seen before."

"What do you even need a tree for anyway? 'Cause you aren't the favourite of the cooks? They'll do anything for you!"

He shrugged.

"'Cause you could."

I looked at Jase in askance. Broad shoulders and a piercing azure gaze stared back at me.

"I can't Create, you know that. It's against the Law."

Jase nodded and broke off half the roll, tossing it to me. White dreadlocks flicked across his shoulders, drifting down his back as he walked.

"Since when have you obeyed the Law?"

"SHHH!" I jabbed him with my elbow, catching the heel of the roll he tossed my way. It was good, still warm. I loved what the cooks could make, but it wasn't the same as being able to Create.

We fell into silence, warmth radiating on my back. I was glad to be free. Glad too, that the Earth had never taken offence at my habit of Creating. I still didn't see what was so bad about it. But I didn't want to rant again, not with Jase around. Besides, he'd heard it all before.

My eyes closed, and I breathed in, expanding my chest. I let it out with a contented sigh, slipped on the damp grass, and toppled over.

Jase caught me, his arm slipping easily around my waist. I leaned into his side.

"Steady there," he murmured, the heat of his

hand resting on the small of my back a moment longer than necessary.

Jase—he got to bind the vines into fantastic shapes, building homes and workplaces for us in whatever style he liked. *Can't Create my*—I snorted again. All I got to do was stick my fingers in the dirt—well, what little we found from natural rock falls where it was deemed sanctuary to take. Sacred Earth.

Just in case we pissed Her off again.

"Still cranky they took you to task?" Jase asked with no small amount of sympathy. *He'd* never been dragged before the Keepers—though his father was one, his younger brother next in line—he had seen me walk out with my head held high, make it to the edge of the forest, and collapse in a shivering heap. Had I cried the last time? That was embarrassing. I armed myself with a grin, showing teeth.

"Nothing they won't say to me next time."

Expecting some cheeky repartee, I tossed the remains of the roll back at Jase. He caught it, studying me with a serious expression. I faltered.

"What?"

It came out a little more aggressive than I had

meant it. Those liquid eyes never left mine, and heat seared my cheeks. I rubbed my neck.

"Next time they might not let you off so easily," he said in a low voice. I checked behind us, but there was no one there. I bit my lip. He was right, but I didn't want to admit it.

"You don't think they'd appreciate some quick-grow mushrooms? Or a batch of bouncing blueberries? What about some fiery chilis," I theorised, imagining the panel of Keepers frantically gulping water, "If I made them just the right size, while they're drowning themselves to take the edge off, we could shove them right up their–"

Jase bellowed with laughter, cutting off the rest of my comment. He stuffed the rest of the roll in his mouth, still speaking around it, but everything came out muffled.

I grinned back, glad to have lightened the mood. I'd be in trouble for it, but for the life of me, I just didn't seem to be able to stop. To be contained. My brow furrowed as I stared out over the forest that edged my greenhouse at the bottom of the hill. A small crowd gathered halfway down, caught my attention. I veered off, sharing a glance with Jase, who followed me.

No one came down here except us, or maybe Nestor when he was bored. A crowd could only mean something bad had happened.

I paused at the edge of the gathering, unsure. I wasn't very good with people—anything I said came out awkward. Being too unpopular with the Keepers hadn't won me any friends either. Jase passed me, tapped a shoulder, and pushed his way through. I followed in his wake.

A cleared area opened out. In the centre was a man, balancing as though on his toes. Jase's hand wrapped around my arm, keeping me behind him. I looked up in surprise. His eyes found mine with an intense gaze, and my stomach clenched, reminiscent of my Bidding. I slipped under his arm, looking harder at the man.

A shaft of some sparkling mineral protruded from his chest, its tip darkened, spreading a stain on the woven material of his shirt. Lifeblood trickled down his frozen form, pooling on the ground where it sank in, a life sucked away.

The ground tremored—a tiny thing that drew a

gasp from those gathered. Not one person moved. *Cowards.* I launched forward, desperate to help. Jase's arms wrapped around my middle, pressing me tightly against him. I struggled to get free until he whispered in my ear.

"You have to let Her have him."

I stilled, my tears leaving little puddles on the tanned forearms tight at my waist. I watched as they dripped slowly to the ground, waiting for the Earth to react. An air of fear permeated the crowd. Would She take us all, or would penance be paid in salt and iron?

A stillness settled over us as the man struggled to breathe, fingers stretched wide, fighting his fate. Life left him with a soft sigh, features set, hands limp. The crowd drifted away, murmuring. Some shot dark glares and frowns my way. We stayed until the last of them were gone, Jase's arms loosening as he turned me to face him.

"I don't want this to happen to you."

"Did you know him?"

A slow nod was my only answer. Of course, he did. Jase knew everyone, and they loved him. He helped out wherever he could while I hid away, tending my plants and hiding my Creations. I wanted to ask about the man's life, what he did, his name. Did he have children, a family now bereft of his comfort in the dark of night? But I couldn't. It felt like prying. Instead, I asked the only question that would come out.

"Why?"

"He liked to dig. Felt like he connected with...with..." He couldn't finish the sentence, so I did it for him.

"The Earth."

He nodded miserably, eyes cast to the ground. I slid into his space, wrapping my arms around his waist. I wondered if he would reject me, but he lifted me higher, holding me to his taut, lean frame. I pressed my cheek to his chest, listening to the solid rhythm of his heart, matching to my own.

After a time, his arms loosened, setting me down gently. Without a word or glance, he trudged across the hillside to my greenhouse. Tears left damp trails on my cheeks when I faced the impaled man, knowing he wouldn't be there in the morning. Even we didn't go to waste. The Earth would dispose of him in Her own way.

I wished I had words, comfort, but there wasn't anything left to give. He had left this world; nothing remained but a cool, empty shell. For a moment, I envied him, free of the stresses we faced daily. I bowed my head, suddenly unsure. I traced Jase's footprints in the wet grass with my weathered boot before turning to follow his steps without looking at the man again.

All thoughts of a day with him were gone. I didn't want him to see what was in my greenhouse. Jase's form retreated, his strides long. I chased after him, not wanting him to be alone in his grief.

He was silent when I reached his side, brushing his hand, but he didn't reach out. The doubt stuck with me, and I wondered if I should have hung back. Then I looked at him, really looked at him. Face tight, jaw clenched. He was suffering as much as I, more, and I knew I was about to make it worse.

He slowed for me, and I matched his steps, thinking of the man, the Keepers, my Bidding. Unease gripped me. What if they were right? Could my Creations lead to the same end? I considered— putting aside my ego for a moment. Creating was just so natural for me. I didn't want to cause harm to these people, my people, no matter how they shunned me. But I had my work, my plants.

I had Jase.

I smiled, his warm presence a comfort in the wake of tragedy. In a small community, one death reminded us there was once an entire world of people. Now, there was just us. People worked well under the Laws, except me and some of the Sky folk. They made their own laws, lived their own way. But it wasn't destructive, didn't incite the wrath of Her. Yet they were Outcast, as the Keepers had threatened me.

Jase's father, Mal, led the Keepers. We didn't get on well. I was always challenging something, trying to do something different than the way they saw the world.

*We should be grateful to have a world.*

The phrase ran through my head. I'd heard it more than once—pretty sure it would be said to me again sometime. Soon, even. Nestor never missed an opportunity to rub it in, how different I was. Why couldn't I just conform like everyone else?

We skittered down the hill to my greenhouse. Panes of squiggly glass reflected white though the rainbows danced above us. I still wasn't sure what Jase had asked the glassmakers to add into the mix to achieve the effect, but I was glad for the extra degree of privacy it afforded me.

A piece of driftwood hanging above the door declared *'Veritas' Ark.'* Jase had carved out the words and presented it to me when I first began working, marking it as a place just for me. He'd added a little squiggle, like an eye in the middle of the 'A.' Watching over me, he said. It creeped me out, but I hadn't the heart to tell him.

I wrapped my fingers around the door handle. It was smooth from use and turned with ease. I needed to ask Jase to fix the lock—old and dodgy to begin with, Jase had scavenged it from some ruin—it had dropped down, making a horrid grating noise when I tried to use it. As though someone had tried to force it, or break in. The thought gave me pause—but who would want to break into my insignificant world?

I turned to ask Jase to fix it—on top of his regular duties; he was an all-around handyman—when his hand clamped down over mine. I jolted, my breath gone; he was much too close.

"Don't do anything else to get their attention, V. They'll take you off duty, put you in the Vault." Worried eyes stared down at me. He was so close. I breathed him in. The warm, forest scent that came from working with the vines every day.

I shook my head at him to break the moment, if nothing else. Jase frowned, far too serious for me. Irritated, I curled my lips back, baring my teeth in a feral smile. It was all I had left in me. I turned the handle and opened the door with a shove of my arm.

"Then wait 'til they see this."

# Chapter Two

I hadn't meant to show anyone, too afraid someone *would* inform the Keepers I'd been at it again. Especially so soon after my recent Bidding. But showing Jase was different.

He filled the entry to my greenhouse; one hand holding the door open, the other braced on the door frame. Lean muscles bunched beneath the soft fabric our weavers made, tendons lacing tanned forearms. He looked too big for such a fragile place, but I knew he wouldn't break anything. After all, he was the one who built it.

For me.

His lips parted, and he inhaled sharply.

"V, what did you *do*?"

The words came out fast, breath hissing along with it. My grin faded, and I followed his gaze as it swept the room with precision, missing nothing.

The greenhouse was a long, slim building; the

delicate glass panes held firm by giant buttress roots Jase had encouraged to grow, thick trunks that framed my gardens, arching overhead. Where light normally shone through was covered with dark green foliage, heart-shaped leaves overly large, just the way I had designed them. But that wasn't what held his attention.

Plants grew out of control all the time. It was the Earth's prerogative, plus his and mine. Our jobs melded, our gifts bordering on sacrilege. I was allowed to cultivate, even cross a few plants together. Jase brought spurts of life to plants, aging them overnight to form beautiful structures. I pollinated what the insects couldn't. But that was where it ended. I wasn't allowed to Create; certainly not like *this*.

Tiny, glowing balls hovered in the air, suspended on thin vines almost invisible in the dim light. One of the Sky People had described a *sun* to me, and I had been determined to make one, even though I knew it would get me into strife.

Jase stared at the mini suns, his hand drifting up to touch one. It bobbed against his skin, and he grinned. I sighed with relief until his eyes flashed at me. I gulped.

"You shouldn't have done this," he growled, voice low enough to send sparks up my spine. I shifted uncomfortably. I hated Jase being angry with me. The corner of his mouth tugged up as he continued playing with the plant. It wrapped around his arm, crawling up to his neck. He batted it away.

"This is too much," he murmured. "You're pushing too far."

"I know," I whispered. I worried my lip between my teeth, then burst out with all my reasons. "If we had a power source other than the glass ovens, there would be so much less time spent on just cooking. We'd be able to warm spaces for young children much easier without using the glass ovens. Plus, we would be able to see at night. A time of quiet to contemplate the day gone, with those you were closest to." I stumbled on the last part, my cheeks heating.

When the rainbows darkened each evening, people grabbed their food to watch the auroras flit about in the twilight. Jase and I often took our fare to a hill just beyond a little copse of trees. It removed us away from the prying eyes of the community. People seemed to respect this and kept their distance.

I still wasn't sure why Jase hung out with me—there were a lot more outgoing girls around, and I was sure he had mates who would rather have had him eat with them. That he wanted to spend time with me meant I wasn't alone. I was grateful for it; I just hoped it wasn't entirely out of sympathy.

Having evening lights meant families could socialise longer without sitting in the dark of their homes. It meant someone like me could keep working. But the Keepers didn't think the way I did. They wouldn't be happy with what I'd done; they'd be furious.

The glow inside my glasshouse was dim and warm, reminiscent of a night full of fireflies. Those and butterflies were the largest creatures to survive the aftermath. I drew Jase into the gloom. He resisted, and I tugged harder on his arm. He shot me a look I couldn't interpret but let me lead him further inside.

I wondered for a moment if I'd made a mistake bringing him here. I glanced up at his hard face, misgivings tightening my stomach. I mean, come on, this was *Jase.* My most ardent defender and occasional co-conspirator. I could always rely on him.

Positioning him before a mini-sun, I brushed my hand against it. It shivered then shot up into the canopy of leaves, each curling back on each other until the glass panels of the roof and walls were exposed to the icy, rainbow light once more.

The corner of his mouth turned up, and I knew he was pleased with my methods. Camouflaging my Creations was safer than trying to hide an entire greenhouse of contraband. Jase played with one of the vines that dangled before him, tracing it across the wall. I let him play, knowing he would come to terms to my surprise better when I didn't interfere.

Leaving him searching for the root, I returned to my seedlings. I collected condensation that ran down the panes in small tubes, feeding them into the rows that needed it most. It wasn't much, but water was scarce, as it always had been. We only used what the Earth gave us, or what we could scavenge without upsetting Her.

It appeared She allowed what I did.

Twisting the tubes, so they dripped into my

newest batch, I tapped back several curious tendrils. This Creation was more active than my last. Even now, they crept their way up the thick vine stalks and onto the tubing. I flapped them away and finished up. I untangled a delicate curl of vine which waggled at me and sprouted new leaves along its length. A light ball popped out at my face.

I waved it away, a little disturbed. It reminded me of an eyeball. A shudder ran through me, giving me pause. I wondered, just for a moment, if the Keepers weren't right after all. Maybe I *was* meddling with things I shouldn't be.

Toting my tools back to the bench near the door, I stumbled on a fresh mound of dirt I was certain hadn't been there before my Bidding. My boot scuffed the heap, and a plant sprung up from the freshly turned soil. I frowned at it. Who knew what these plants were up to when I wasn't there to supervise their shenanigans. Next, they'd be hosting pot-plant parties.

I glanced around, hoping Jase hadn't seen my discomfort, certain he would try to talk me out of any more Creating. The bottom line was that I didn't *want* to stop. I was having too much fun. Dirt tracked down a pane of glass, and I spotted him halfway up one of the larger buttresses at the opposite end of the greenhouse, one leg wrapped around the heavy vine, the other braced on a tabletop examining the vine where it had retreated.

I stepped over a long vine with a criss-cross diamond pattern on it—*that was a lot smaller yesterday*—and handed him a bunch of ties, grinning. He just couldn't help himself. While he was discovering a new species of plant, Jase was also in full design mode, twinning the tendrils together, curling them around the structural vines. Intricate patterns swept across the glass panes. Rainbow light shone through the gaps where he had plaited seven strands of vines together, creating shadows on the dirt floor.

"It's beautiful," I murmured, running my hands over them. Not one vine was bent or bruised. He had a talent with the plants, more than I ever had in this way, as though he communicated with them.

If I tried to plait event three strands together, I'd snap off one and spend the week apologising to the plant in terror I'd start a new war with the Earth. I had no such qualms in creating new plants, new life.

Jase completed his design and bounced down from the table, landing lightly next to me. Another skill I'd never mastered. Maybe the next stained-glass window should be of him, I mused, thinking of the cat. I shuddered. Jase gave a throaty laugh.

"What?" Jase was staring down at me, a lopsided grin on his face.

"You've outdone yourself, Ver. This is incredible. But you know–"

"The Keepers will hate it. Yeah." I muttered, giving him a shove. Broad chested as he was, he didn't so much as sway. He grinned down at me, reaching out to snag my waist. My hands hit his chest. I was unsure if I wanted to push him away or pull him closer. He bent his head, and his lips grazed my ear.

"We have to find a way to hide this, somehow."

*Hide what? Oh, the plants. Get a grip, V.* I nodded.

"The Keepers will hate it," I sighed. "But–," I was interrupted before I could finish the thought. A new voice penetrated the damp atmosphere inside my greenhouse.

"The Keepers will hate what?"

Jase and I whirled around together, facing the

doorway. A dark shape filled it, lean but imposing.

*Nestor.*

Swathed in a long coat, he leaned against the doorway, hands in pockets, gaze on me. Muscles bunched in my back, a shiver coursing down my spine. Warm fingers squeezed my waist, making me glad I wasn't alone.

*I am in so much trouble.*

The chance of keeping my Creation a secret was long gone. I took a deep breath, considering what to say for an instant. It would be helpful if some snazzy repartee came out, but I doubted it. I was never very good under pressure.

My lips parted as Jase lifted me off my feet, placing himself between my enemy and me. A protective stance. I was not ungrateful for the gesture, but this was my mess to fix. I squeezed Jase's arm and pressed firmly down.

"What are you doing here?"

It was a blunt question aimed at Nestor. My greenhouse was a private space for me to work in, usually alone. *Mine.* One of the few things I could claim. But Nestor and I hadn't seen eye to eye since we were six years old when he had thrown a hive of wasps at me and run off laughing.

Black hair flopped over one side of his face as he lounged against the glass. I hated that. If I couldn't see someone's eyes, I couldn't read their expression, and that bugged me—what were they hiding? In Nestor's case, usually everything.

"Do mine ears deceive me? You've Created something that will annoy the Keepers again? Really." His words dripped sarcasm.

Wrestling me for front space, Jase growled. It was an amazingly sexy sound. Nestor smirked at me.

The vines and their mini-suns had retracted at his entrance, removing the evidence. I smiled inwardly at the idea of my plants protecting me, or themselves. Then I looked at the hulking figure, still pressing me back, and decided the plants could fend for themselves right now.

I stepped back, letting Jase win the wrestling competition. His head whipped around, grinning at me. I grinned back, but it faded as he faced Nestor. A pity Nestor saw it. His lips curved as his gaze contacted mine, sending an unpleasant tremor through my body. Jase must have felt it as he shuddered in response, his arm still contacting mine. He stretched, commanding the space around us with impressive ease.

"What do you want?" He glared at Nestor.

"Oh dear, this is one you might think of distancing yourself from, you know." Nestor flicked one of the leaves, and it struck back, curling around his finger. A glowing ball popped out at him, and the same disquiet exploded in my stomach. *These weren't ready for show.* So much for keeping a secret.

"Intriguing," he murmured, tracing the outline of the leaf. It curved back, exposing its surface. His gaze lanced through me; I quailed beneath it. Jase reached back, slinking an arm around me, holding me up.

"You're okay," he murmured.

Nestor smiled, a horrible thing. "It's alright, *brother,* I'm off now." He threw that stomach curdling smile over his shoulder as he departed. "Off to have lunch with Father."

*You bastard.*

Nestor grinned and tugged on one of the mini-suns. He flicked away the vine he'd played with before. It shivered, pulling back to hover above him. He didn't see it stretch to slide into his hair, frolicking with the strands from behind. I suppressed a grin.

"You short on entertainment?" Jase braced an arm on a buttress above my head. I breathed in the scent of him with my eyes closed. As I opened them, I realised Nestor was still staring at me. I glared back.

His tongue ran across the tips of his teeth, and I shuddered—this time in disgust. Jase turned his head to look at me. I wasn't sure whether his expression was intrigued or defensive. A muscle jumped in his jaw, and suddenly there were too many people in my greenhouse. My fingers curled into fists at my sides. This was meant to be *my* space.

"Get out." The command came from Jase before I could sound out the words, but they were the same. I smiled at him in appreciation, but the sentiment was lost; he was staring at his brother. Nestor shrugged and made a show of leaving, flamboyantly bowing his way out.

I clenched my teeth until they ground together

audibly. Jase winced.

"Not the prettiest habit, right?" I mumbled the words, embarrassed I had let Nestor get to me. I smirked to cover my discomfort.

"Just think of me as the newest resident of the Vault."

Jase didn't respond for a moment. I gabbled on. "I'm sure I can entertain the other inmates with fantastical stories, or even maybe listen to some of theirs, whadda you–,"

'You'll be the *only* inmate." Jase growled.

*Oh.*

He grabbed my hand, towing me along.

"Where are we going?"

"I'm taking you to see the Sky People."

# CHAPTER THREE

I trotted after Jase up the lawn. He dragged me to the top of the hill with his longer strides. I had an inkling of where he was leading me, but it didn't make me happy. I trusted Jase to keep me safe from other people; I was too awkward with company, and he knew I had little care for my own reputation amongst the community. We entered the forest with its dark shadows and creaking boughs. Though I knew there was nothing to fear in it, I kept close behind Jase, following a path only he could see. I wondered how many times he had come this way. Fortunately, we passed through the forest faster than I had expected.

Beneath the canopy of the trees, I was hidden, sheltered. Safe. The moment I stepped out of the treeline, I'd be exposed. I swallowed, staring down the hill. Below us, a small encampment of rounded huts was barely visible through the foliage at the edge of the forest. Similar to large boulders, the domed huts had been fitted with glass lenses stacked one upon the other set into the sides of the roof. Rumour had it the occupants stared through the holes in their domes at the rainbows dancing above, discussing worlds no one else knew about or remembered.

The Sky People were different, even more so than I was. They were as close to the edge of being Outcast without the law actually being applied to them. Separate from our little community, they bartered with those few who accepted them. The Keepers saw to it they were not with us for evening fare, but from what Jase had told me, the Sky People preferred their own evening ritual.

What no one would tell me was why—what it was they saw through their lenses that were so fascinating? What kept them separate from the rest of society? I wanted to find out. But they were such a tight society that the rest of us—especially trouble-makers like me—were excluded from their group.

It appeared fear went both ways.

Jase, on the other hand, with his keen

intelligence and open heart, was welcome everywhere. My heart tugged for a moment, reminding me how apart I was from our community. Jase's presence kept me inside the edge—*just*—of acceptable society. Without him, I would have already been in the Vault. Or worse, Outcast.

I shuddered to think what life would be like on the outskirts, in the forest. The wilds stretched beyond the view of our tallest hill—we didn't have anything that qualified as a mountain, though I knew explorers from previous generations had discovered them.

Noone left the community under their own steam. It was an unwritten law, agreed between our people. Don't do anything to anger the Earth. Don't leave the settlement. Don't Create. If I were Outcast, foraged fruits would sustain me, but that was all. With our temperate climate, I wouldn't die until I was old. Unless I pissed off the Earth, I would just *survive*.

That's what the Earth gave us. A prison. A place to live, to exist. Unless we harmed ourselves—well, history, even our stunted, verbal one—taught us to steer clear of that path. Survive was all we could do. But to be alone—truly alone—was enough to break any mind. For all my bluster about not caring, expulsion would finish me.

We stepped out of the forest onto the grass. I was suddenly exposed, open to whatever hurt would come at me. I was better steering clear of people in general, hiding in my greenhouse. My fingers wrapped tighter around Jase's hand and tugged with a sudden need to go back. Then I thought of Nestor and the threat he posed to my livelihood and stopped. If these people could help in any way, I would be grateful.

Jase tossed a grin over his shoulder, drawing me along with him. I smiled back but refused to trot behind him any longer. A few quick strides caught me up to him before we reached the carved stone huts.

We approached the largest hut, situated just off centre of a ring of domed buildings, and Jase rapped loudly on the door. I cringed a little, wanting to be far away from this group of people. His fingers tightened around mine. I squeezed back as the door opened. A tall, lithe woman stood there in long grass robes, looking for all the world just like the rest of us.

As soon as her eyes lit on Jase, a smile filled her gaunt face, and she exclaimed in welcome. Her thin arms enfolded him. She was of an equal height with him; it was unusual for a woman to be so tall.

Her eyes opened, looking directly into mine over Jase's shoulder. The corners of her mouth thinned, and she stepped back from Jase to look fully into his face. He shrugged. I imagined the goofy expression he often pulled to get out of trouble, even though I couldn't see his face.

Whatever it was worked for him yet again, but the woman still frowned at me as she gestured us into her home. I ducked under her arm into a bright, well-lit room covered in floor mats and pillows. A wonderful aroma filled the cosy space. It was well past dinner. With a start, I realized we were intruding on their mealtime. The day had aged while we walked through the forest. I tugged on Jase's sleeve.

"We should go," I murmured.

"We're fine." He drew me into the closed space, interlacing our fingers—to stop me escaping? He drew me to his side, clearing his throat.

"Sandrine, this is Veritas. She is open to learning from your wisdom."

Was I? He glanced over his shoulder at me, eyebrows raised in silent question. Just for him, I nodded, attempting a smile. It came out watery. The look on Sandrine's face told me she knew exactly who I was, and who had dragged me here. She sighed and motioned us inside.

In a room devoid of plant life, I began to freak out, just a little. Small spaces were not my friend. But the Sky People had managed to bring the outside indoors. Lit candles scented with gardenia burned on curved shelves. Chatter filled the space, bouncing off the walls. Vegetable curry in bowls was set out upon a long bench, for many more than were in the hut. I turned back to Sandrine, speaking before I thought.

"Were you expecting us?"

She stared at me for a long moment. I twitched uncomfortably beneath her gaze, wishing I'd kept my mouth shut. Her eyes narrowed, brows drawing in. Finally, she broke the impasse, nodding at Jase.

"I expected you to come to us."

Done with me, she stepped away, collecting bowls on her arm and passing them around. When she reached me, she hesitated, as though not wanting to share food with me. I didn't reach to take one from her; instead, I looked her full in the face.

"Why?"

Her head twitched, as though she sought to escape. I held her gaze, refusing to back down. A light finger touched my arm. It was Jase's request for me to be kind—after all, he had brought me here for help, and he knew how defensive I could be. I inclined my head in his direction, a tiny motion, and waited.

"We were…once like you." She extended a bowl, and I took it by reflex, a little dumbfounded she was willing to speak to me.

My stomach rumbled. Whatever they had done to the curry, it smelled amazing. Sandrine moved on, passing out more bowls. Friends greeted each other, seating themselves on cushions piled high, squeezing in next to one another. Physical contact appeared to be natural to these people, almost as if they required it. I twitched, slightly uncomfortable in such a crowded space.

Used to eating outside at our regular haunt, I searched for a vacant spot in the pillows. A small pile of unoccupied cushions sat between two groups of Sky People clustered together. I wiggled into the pillows, trying not to pitch backwards.

I got comfortable and spooned the thick sauce into my mouth. Heaven. Spices and herbs jumped out at me, dredging visions of my greenhouse with its damp soil and fragrant leaves. My spoon scraped the bottom of the bowl, surprising me.

I swallowed my last mouthful and tuned back into the room. There was a pleasant quietness to the small space, crowded as it was. The dim light and low murmur of sporadic conversation gave an ambience of warmth and safety. *Acceptance.* Something I hadn't felt in...well, I couldn't remember the last time.

Maybe when I still had a family. Their faces swam in my blurred vision, and I looked down at my hands, away from the room. Suddenly, I craved privacy again. I hadn't realised how easy it was to feel lonely in a room full of people.

My cushion dipped, and a warm body shunted me sideways. I rocked off balance for a moment, clutching the bowl. I was terrified of shattering it on the stone floor. Jase parked himself solidly at my back, and I righted myself against him.

His arm wrapped around my waist, and he stared at me with those intense eyes. Stripped bare, all my secrets were exposed under that gaze. Strangely, it didn't feel intrusive; I was safe with him. His blue eyes deepened in the dimmed light. I resisted the urge to press my fingers against his cheek, knowing I'd feel stubble there.

He battled to balance his bowl on his knees and eat one-handed until I nudged his arm. He just shook his head, looking determined. Laughing, I propped his bowl up with my hand. He gave me a happy smile and dug in.

His bowl emptied as fast as mine had. Unlike mine, his bowl got a refill—to the brim. My stomach rumbled again in protest, and I eagerly took a piece of flatbread as a basket was passed around from group to group.

Soft chatter filled the dome. I tilted my head back, gazing through the holes in the roof. Frozen auroras glinted across the darkened space, but nothing new jumped out at me. What I was supposed to be seeing that kept this little community apart from the rest of us escaped me. No great rift or bubble in the skyscape showing new worlds presented itself.

This was the same sky I stared at throughout the day—what was so different about it? I was still in awe of this outcast world—separate but together. Saddened for a moment at the thought of never being part of something special like this, I rubbed my neck, rotating it side to side where it was sore from craning to the sky. I lowered my gaze to ground level to find nigh on thirty people staring at me.

I froze, too startled to blink. The moment stretched on. Cramps formed in my feet as I tensed but didn't dare wriggle. Then a grin formed on the man's face straight across from me, and he began to laugh. It was contagious, passing from person to person until the entire dome echoed with the laughter of its people.

Arching my feet to relieve the knots, I looked around, seeing only the unity these people held. Even Jase laughed, his broad frame rocking against my side. A pang of loneliness struck me again. It must have reflected in my face, as the man across from me let his laughter fade to a smile, motioning at the ceiling. He said something, but I couldn't hear above the conversation that filled the room.

Seeing I couldn't hear him, he gestured again to the roof, then back to the floor. My brow creased with the effort to follow him. He pointed again to the floor, jabbing the air harder, then punching a cushion. He stretched his hand wide in a gliding motion over the pillow, then back to the hole in the roof.

Comprehension hit me in the face. I was supposed to lie down and look up to the sky. Oops. I managed a grin and mimed smacking myself in the forehead. He grinned, giving me a thumbs up and turned back to his friends—likely to tell them how silly the new girl was. I huffed a small laugh. At least I'd gotten the point in the end.

I pivoted around to find a bemused Jase looking straight at me. I blinked in surprise, wary of anything else I'd done that might be considered humorous, shaking my head and shrugged at him—adrift.

"Nothing," he said softly.

A shuffling sound caught my attention. Around me, people settled, finishing up their conversations. I cocked an eyebrow at Jase and turned back.

Sandrine stood in the centre of the room. Her robes flowed to the ground. In her hands, she held a large, fat candle. A chill breeze blew through the open windows above, and the flame guttered. I started, worried for a moment the woman's dress would catch fire, but it didn't, and I settled with the rest of the group.

I hadn't known that my life lacked music until she began to sing. Nothing I'd ever heard compared. Lilting notes filled the room. People swayed in the dim light, and a hum arose, deep notes complementing her higher tones. I closed my eyes, letting the music weave its way around me.

My mind filled with memories I shunted away, replaced by scents of the forest, damp mulch beneath bare feet, laughing up at Jase in the light streaming through the canopy. It seemed an age, but when the music ended, I fought to open my eyes.

I wasn't tired; I was more awake than I could ever remember being. The music had sated something empty inside me. I breathed deeply through my nose as the woman placed her hand directly over the flame, smothering it. The room fell dark.

"The music of the planets," Jase murmured in my ear, so close his breath was warm where it brushed across my neck. I shivered despite the sultry air from so many people huddled together.

Pillows shifted, rustling sounded in the dark. Mine got yanked out from beneath me, and I made a small squawk as I toppled to the ground. A deep chuckle came from somewhere above me, and large hands gently squeezed my shoulders, pressing me backwards. I resisted him for a moment, unsure. Jase pushed again, and I leaned back.

A pillow caught my head, and I nestled into it, sorting myself around to lie beneath the nearest window. Jase lay back on the cushion next to me, brushing his fingers over mine. A small shock went through me, and I squeezed back.

A grating noise broke the moment. In the windows, twin rounds of glass, smoother and clearer than I'd seen, slotted themselves across the circular gap.

I wondered how they operated. Jase wordlessly pointed to a man standing at the wall, pressing down on something. I guessed he was using a level of fallen timber to manipulate the glass somehow. But glass like that—even my greenhouse's glass panels—had ripples through the largest ones, the world outside faceted. None were as clear as these.

There was only one way I fathomed the glass panels could exist—Creation. If every one of the domed huts held glass like this... I was beginning to see why Jase had brought me here.

Through the glass, I could see a white patch in the frozen sky sphere which turned out not to be a bubble, but rather a large crack in the ice. I shivered again—in fear this time—as Jase described what we were seeing. The thought of all that ice raining down on us—I could only imagine the devastation it would cause. Perhaps it wasn't the Earth we should be afraid of, but the Sky. A question formed on my lips—I had so many already, I barely knew where to start—when Jase shushed me. He placed a finger over my lips, brushing them down my cheek, then pointed above.

I closed my mouth and looked back at the sky. I

hoped I wouldn't forget anything important about tonight. A third glass slid into place—this one had circular ripples around the edges and a wide space in the centre. The sky suddenly seemed closer, and I wondered if the third glass was curved.

In the centre of the lenses, a black dot appeared. As the last glass slotted into place, the dot expanded to encompass the entirety of the three lenses. Inside the glass was a world of its own. Dazzling bright lights, sharp as gems in sunlight decorated a deep black that went on forever. I held onto the ground to stop myself from falling in. Jase covered my hand with his own, and I felt steadier.

Rainbows danced on the walls, enhanced by the lenses. I felt small as Sandrine again began to sing, telling the story of the stars, the planets, the sun.

My world expanded as I learned about our solar system—theories about the universe beyond. My eyes went wide when Jase explained all they had discovered and how much the Sky People wanted to pass their knowledge on but was held back by the Keepers of the Law. Knowledge of what it meant to be truly free, from societal boundaries, from the cage of the Earth wrapped around us, imprisoning us on our own world.

I knew then; without a doubt, I had been correct. The Sky People had been Creating, just like me. A smile curved my lips. I turned my head to Jase. He was still pointing out constellations, telling their stories with eyes bright as a child's. I leaned closer.

"Thank you," I whispered.

Jase grinned, pressing his forehead to mine.

# Chapter Four

A while later, Sandrine relit the candles. Groups formed again on the cushions, chattering quietly. Two people joined us, and to my surprise, a woman I'd never met leant over to hug me.

"Welcome," she whispered softly.

Tea was passed around. I inhaled, the zing of ginger shooting up my nose. One person from each group poured the tea into small, earthen-fired cups. I was surprised when Jase poured for our group. He murmured something over the cups and passed them out. I took mine, and the cup warmed my hands. The aroma was sharp enough to wake me, and I was startled to realise I didn't know how much time had passed.

"So…" Jase took his cup and sat back. "What did you think?"

The small group focused on me, alight with curiosity though it was hidden well behind gazes used to prejudice.

"It was," I paused, searching for the right word and coming up empty. "Astounding. Amazing. Mind-blowing. Mind-*opening*." Many words make up for the lack of the perfect one, right? I blushed, mortified to sound so lacking when these people had displayed an intelligence greater than all the Keepers in the Hall.

The two gentle faces opposite me nodded, and I gave a shy smile as more people joined our circle. Being the centre of attention wasn't my forte; I didn't do people. Jase knew that. I began to count the faces in our group.

Teacups clinked onto serving plates. Quiet goodbyes filled the dome as the Sky People filtered out into the evening air. Soon, our group was the only one left.

The last person was seated, and Jase poured for us all. For a brief moment in my life, I was part of a group. It was such an odd feeling; I didn't even consider it as I held out my cup for a refill. Jase smiled as he tipped the teapot, not quite emptying it of aromatic liquid.

He placed the pot in the centre of the circle. It

amazed me that in a large space, people pressed themselves together, clustered in tight groups. For defence, comfort? I didn't know. But for the first time, I felt safe, and it wasn't because Jase was there. I wasn't abnormal; a freak shunned as I so often was within our usual community.

I was *accepted* here.

The faces around me glowed bronze, a sign of working outside, like Jase. I was pale in comparison; my days and evenings spent in my greenhouse, rather than exposed to the direct light of the skyscape. Questions tingled the tip of my tongue, but I didn't know where to begin. The stars, the *moon*—that one got me, something so big so close to us, but so far, both physically and mentally. I wondered what the Keepers would have made of this knowledge, and the question stuck with me. *Did they know?*

Is that what our lives were to be—distant from each other, though so near? Like the Sky People to us. I had seen nothing tonight that justified their diminished social status.

My tea finished, I placed my cup on the tray with the pot, nodding thanks to both Jase and our host.

Jase nudged my shoulder with his.

"Maybe next time you can pour."

My eyes must have been as wide as the pot because the rest of our little congregation laughed.

"I– I– I couldn't, I mean…" I stammered and trailed off, a wee bit flabbergasted at being offered—well, anything. A grin split Jase's face.

"It's not what you think," he scooted over to me, lifting the pot. "It's a heavy thing; you'll need both hands." He demonstrated, wrapping my hands around the near-empty pot. I wriggled a little at his nearness in front of people—any people—but especially those that I didn't even know their names.

"You pour, try not to spill any," I turned my head up to look into his laughing eyes—the bugger knew *exactly* how uncomfortable this made me. "It's about serving," he went on in a more serious note. "It's not about being the biggest, or best in the group, but being the smallest, the very least. Wanting to serve," he finished with a small flourish, placing the pot and cups back on the tray.

I nodded, unsure I'd be able to do that for anyone else. Jase wiggled out of the circle, managing to stand without dropping anything, tray displayed on one arm. He placed it on one of the curved shelves decorating the hut and seated himself next to me. "It's about letting others be bigger than yourself," he murmured, tucking stray hairs behind my ear.

I wondered briefly if it were a rebuke, but took his speech on humbleness to heart. Perhaps I shouldn't worry so much of what people thought—Jase was the only one who knew I really *did* care about others' opinions—I just hid it well behind bluster and stunts like today's mini -suns, which brought me back to the point.

"Were you outcast for Creating the lenses?" I asked bluntly. Subtlety *not* being my thing. Jase frowned at his pillow, and gasps echoed around the circle. So maybe I could have said that a little better.

Sandrine's face was blank as she seated herself next to the girl who had hugged me earlier.

"The lenses *were* Created, but not by us."

Her voice had a soft lilt as though she were on the edge of breaking into song again.

"He was Outcast too, long ago." Her lashes caressed her cheeks as she closed her eyes. For a moment, I wondered if I would see tears. Just the thought discomforted me. Losing my mask of cool in company embarrassed me—I could only imagine what it might mean to cry in the presence of others to a person with such dignity.

"He sought knowledge, the only way we can here."

Her eyes bore directly into mine, as though sending me a message. But we had no knowledge, bar that passed from elder generations to younger. Skills and stories learned by word of mouth and experience. Except for those books that were frozen.

I paused, staring into those eyes that so resembled Jase's.

"The Library." Words left my mouth before I'd fully considered the implications. Her eyes lit up, and she nodded. It wasn't an approving gesture, more one of victory. Growing up with Nestor made me hate the thought of being manipulated. She'd tempted me, and I'd bitten. For the second time that day, I felt very small.

"What did he—did you—learn?"

So came the story of our past. Of how one man had sent life into the clouds and covered the world with death. Of how one child stopped the storm and froze the sky. Of how the Earth fought back.

All this information, our *history*, could have been made freely available. But the Keepers had frozen our books behind a wall of ice. Safer for the rest of us, to have no knowledge of our past.

*Why?*

I couldn't form the words in my mouth to ask the question. But something happened to those people—a generation lost, a line that disappeared, taking the mystery of what had happened to our world with it.

It all came together in my mind—I had to read those books.

Shy of breaking in and breaking them out, assuming you could read the ancient pages, you needed to be allowed into the Library. Which meant their Outcast had once been the Librarian.

The breath left my chest. I wondered if he had brought texts back to the stone huts to read or shared the knowledge with his people in our traditional storytelling manner – but this was long ago, and the stone huts were recent. So their Librarian had been outcast before I was born. Was this, then, the reason for the Sky People's separation from our society??

I inclined my head in query. She nodded. The air had grown heavy during our silent conversation. I wasn't sure why she was exposing their closest held secrets, especially to me. What was I supposed to do with this information? Did she want me to break into the Library, or befriend her? Friendship wasn't my strong suit, any better than tact.

I shot a guilty glance at Jase. He sat still and quiet, watching me absorb everything I'd heard tonight. I hoped he realised it was a miracle I wasn't freaking out and running screaming from the huts. After all, I had enough problems of my own making to deal with, unless…

"I spend a lot of time with the Keepers," I said, choosing my words with care. "Soon, maybe," Jase jerked in my peripheral vision, but my gaze never wavered from Sandrine's. "They might require me to be…relocated?"

Her head tilted, eyes considering. Finally, she smiled.

"Perhaps the Keepers might consider service…in the Library, perhaps your penance, instead of incarceration? It is much better suited to you as a form of discipline. We will...make suggestions. It is also customary that they listen to the requests of those sentenced with a heavier burden."

A grin spread unbidden across my face. We had a plan.

# Chapter Five

Jase strode out of the hut after wishing everyone a brief good evening, with a hug for Sandrine. I gave a hasty goodbye, thanking Sandrine, and caught up with him halfway up the hill, hands stuffed in his pockets against the cool air, head bowed.

"Wait," I puffed, stopping at the top of the rise just behind him. Jase stopped, too, but didn't turn around.

"You just couldn't help it, could you?" His growl so low I wouldn't have heard it if I hadn't been standing next to him. "You take something special, something beautiful," he swung round to face me, his movement so sudden I took a quick step back. His eyes blazed. It took me a moment to recognise anger. Jase ploughed on before I could open my mouth. "You turn it into something about *you*. Always you." He muttered, the forest at his back. In the dim light, he was little more than a shadow, a sentinel on the hill.

I pursed my lips, waiting for a retort, but nothing came—mostly because he was right. I looked at the ground and kicked a pebble. It ricocheted down the slope sending little eddies of dust swirling into the cool evening air.

"I'm sorry," I whispered, startled as tears pricked the corners of my eyes. For a girl who never cried, I seemed to be doing it a lot recently. Tonight Jase had shown me something special. He had gone out on a limb, bringing me to a place, a people he clearly cherished. It upset me that I might have ruined that for him. "Really," I added to his huff as he stared out over the huts.

"You're right. It was special—*is* special. Amazing. All those people, separate from the rest of us because they are true to what they believe in, what they know." Jase finally turned to stare down at me with hard eyes. "Is it...is it what you worry might happen to me? Outcast?" I stumbled over the last word.

His gaze softened, and he tugged me into his side, warm arms enveloping me. He leaned his chin on my head, turning me to see the little village beneath the rise. The collection of huts sat in a circular shape, with a larger one off-centre, where we had viewed the stars together. My chin dipped as I studied them.

"Cepheus."

Jase tightened his arms around me. I half turned, comprehension dawning.

"The constellation. It's Cepheus, the man with the crazy wife who boasted her daughter was more beautiful. That was the story of Sandrine's song. They built the huts in remembrance, didn't they?"

Or in protest? I fell silent, looking back at the huts aglow in the darkness like the stars they represented.

"You listened."

I smacked his arm with the heel of my hand. His muscles flexed but didn't release me.

"*Of course,* I listened. I *do* do that occasionally." I grinned. "I knew you brought me here for a reason."

Jase shifted his arms, capturing my hand in his larger one.

"They're an eye-opener." He considered me, and I squirmed a little beneath his heavy gaze. " But what they have to say is valid for...our future.

C'mon, I'll take you home."

The walk through the forest didn't take as long as I remembered it had on the way there. Every step reminded me of the wilderness that could become my home if I pushed too hard at my Bidding. Which was certain to come, now Nestor was involved. My stomach dipped. I'd been stupid to Create, but I couldn't help it. The urge in me was far too great. I shivered in the sudden cold, nausea rising in my throat. Sweat broke out on my arms, and my teeth began to chatter.

I turned my face from him, trying to hide the fear that rose in me. I didn't want him worried about me more than he already was; it was my future after all, not his. The thought of us never eating together for our evening meal, showing him something new and *stupid* I'd Created…why did I have to be so careless, so selfish? I squeezed my eyes shut but couldn't stop the tears from coming.

Hands clutched mine, squeezing hard. Inhaling deeply through my nose, I opened my eyes to a blurred shape squatting before me. As my vision cleared, Jase's panicked face came into view. He looked so cute and sweet hovering there; I gave a little giggle. The panic in his eyes shifted from wariness to concern.

"Breathe, V," he encouraged. I giggled harder until suddenly, I lay crumpled in an exhausted heap, barely able to lift my hands.

"Sorry," I whispered, attempting a smile. It didn't feel as though my lips moved, and Jase's expression never changed.

"What happened?" he asked, voice soft, as though not wanting to disturb something dangerous. I shrugged it off and tried to stand. My legs turned to jelly, the world swimming around me.

"The Bidding. Because it's got to come, right? Nestor will be the pain in my ass; he always has been." I sighed and flopped back down.

"You're okay?" Jase still looked slightly panicked. I tried for a smile again, and this time it worked. He smiled back, looking reassured. "I've never seen anything like that."

"What, me have a panic attack about seeing the Keepers again? Nah, I hold those back 'til you go home."

Jase stared at me with those blue eyes turned

dark and disquiet roiled in my chest. I was missing something.

"What?"

Jase rose and stepped back, bringing me to my feet. My breath caught in my throat. Around me, droplets of water hung suspended in the air; perfect, tiny orbs of dew. Worlds encased within themselves. I poked one, fascinated when the water depressed in and bounced back when I removed my hand. Jase looked unnerved, his features stretched tight. His hand was halfway up to touch a drop, but stopped, frozen with indecision.

"V...this is *really* Creating. More. It's..." he struggled to find the right word. "It's Creation."

My lips curved in, and I prodded the bubble again, fascinated.

"Oops?" I offered up a too-bright smile that Jase didn't return. I crossed the few steps between us, laying my hand on his arm. He flinched. I froze, horrified. He didn't move away, just stared at me. Great, so I was only a minor monster. I walked out of the field of water droplets, suddenly wanting to get home. Tonight had fried my mind with an information overload. I needed to be in my greenhouse, staring at the auroras, to process everything I'd learned.

I turned back to Jase.

"Are you coming?"

He just nodded and stayed put. I sighed.

"Oh, come on, it's still me." I flapped my hands in exasperation. The water droplets plunged to the ground, bursting on whatever they hit, including Jase. A very wet man stared at me, water dripping from his fingers, damp strands of hair hanging over his eyes. He inhaled sharply, and I got ready for— well, whatever was coming. He'd never yelled at me before.

Instead, he laughed, a rumble that began somewhere deep inside his chest, bursting out. It echoed around the clearing, disappearing into the shadows. Relieved, I was glad to have back the Jase I understood. I shot back across the clearing, wrapping my arms around his neck, not caring how wet I got.

We parted ways at the top of the hill. I headed down to my greenhouse, thinking of my bed snuggled between two large buttress roots. If I lie flat on my back, I could watch the auroras flicker about until I drifted off. Jase had designed the roots with a large opening directly above my bed. It was a beautiful gesture. I never felt alone at night.

I trotted down the hill, slipping a little on the damp grass. Dew had already begun to form on the tiny blades. The door stood ajar, and I frowned, certain I'd closed it when we'd left. I stepped cautiously inside the greenhouse, tugging on one of the mini-suns for light.

Dozens of tiny balls glowed, illuminating the space nicely. Everyone should have one of these. Life would be so much easier. I checked around the pots and aisles to ensure no surprises were waiting for me there. Nestor popping out at me while I was getting undressed was *definitely* not something I'd fantasized about—wrong brother right there.

Jase, on the other hand...

The aisles were clear. No lurking men in my greenhouse. I sighed, cheeks heating as I thought of Jase, wishing that just for once, I hadn't left him at the top of the hill. I shook my head and refused to let my mind go there. I had too much going on without worrying about any more complications in my life.

As it turned out, I didn't need anything to distract me. A pale sheet of reed paper stood out against the dark wood of my bedroom door. A quick scan confirmed my fears.

My Bidding was in two days.

# CHAPTER SIX

Fresh tendrils curled around the handle of my baskets, passing them to me with amazing dexterity. I took them absently, surveying the foliage covering the roof. My new plant had almost doubled in size overnight, more mini-suns bobbing around me as I packed to head down to the ravine.

Perhaps collecting the glass would show how willing I was to work on my bad habits and would reduce my sentence at my next Bidding. I cringed, pushing the thought aside. I would stay in the present to reduce the chance of another display like the one in the forest last night. If the Keepers got wind of what else I could do—even inadvertently— there was no chance I wouldn't be Outcast—or sentenced to the Vault. Or whatever was worse than those two.

I slipped out the door, heading around the forest to the ravine. It was a decent walk, and after the forest, I tackled another hill, sliding on shale. I reached the edge, tiny leaf fossils skittering into the dark below. A great rent in the earth's surface, the ravine was deep and grey, the place lightning had struck most inland during the Last Storm. Giant granite blocks covered the steep sides, making descent far too steep and unpredictable for my liking.

I made my way to the bottom of the ravine, listening for any indication I was about to be buried alive in a landslide. Silence lay heavy in an area destitute of life. I was lucky this time, not to have to dodge falling rocks. Venturing deeper down a path I'd marked out before, I thought of the Earth, and how angered She must have been to take a life yesterday. Had it only been yesterday? We were so few, though I was sure our numbers meant more to us that it did to Her.

I checked the ground for movement as I walked, wondering if I would end like that—impaled on a spear of granite or sucked into the debris that scattered the ground, drawn into the earth until no trace of me remained. Maybe I would remain a hand or head above the surface, the evidence I had finally drawn Her wrath, and suffered for it.

Shale rained on my head. I ducked by reflex, squawking in fear that my fantasies were about to become reality. I scrambled forward, away from where I thought the rocks would fall. A laugh echoed in the dreary space. I spun around, sighting Nestor standing on a small outcrop, smirking down at me. I glared at him in disgust.

"What are you doing here?"

"Supervising."

"Supervi– what, me?"

Dark eyebrows waggled in my direction. I turned my back to him with a groan, disgruntled. Now, not only did I have to deal with being in a creepy place, but the Keepers also didn't trust me to carry out my sentence.

"Why don't you get down here and start helping?"

"Me, help a vapid-minded klutz like you?"

"A vapid-minded *what?*"

"Just quoting my father." Nestor grinned down at me, apparently enjoying my fury. I muttered under my breath about what his father could do with his opinions, and Nestor too.

"Like father, like son." I snapped, hating that I couldn't help but hurl an insult back.

"Tsk, you'll never learn if you don't do these things yourself."

"Maybe *you* shouldn't have stuck your nose in where it doesn't belong!"

Our snarking carried me through filling one basket of glass and halfway through the second. Stretching tight muscles from crouching over for so long, I looked around. Glass was scarce on the ground. I'd need to go deeper into the ravine if I wanted the task done before midday.

The gorge narrowed a little way along. Some points were tight, and I needed to squeeze through, passing my basket overhead to get into the next section. Above the pinch, the walls of the ravine were so close little light filtered through.

Climbing up a little, I slid my basket onto a ledge. Nestor gave me a cheerful wave. I scowled back. My shoulders went through the pinch first. It took a good bit of wiggling and contorting to get my hips and legs around the rock.

*I'd hate to have to do this in a hurry.*

Balancing my basket, I lowered it carefully to the

ground. If I dropped it, most of the tubes would break. That would be a disaster. It was already close to noon, and I hadn't brought food. I was keen to get out of the ravine as soon as I could.

Darkness blanketed me, closing in. I shivered, scratching at the ground to find the glass, but there was nothing there. I must have picked this area clean last time. I edged deeper into the gloom, clutching my basket.

"Still alive in there?" Nestor's voice bounced around the tiny space. A scatter of pebbles cascaded over me.

"Shut up!" I hissed back, scrabbling about for as many bits of glass as I could. Finally, the basket was full. Nestor called out again, but I ignored him. Rocky walls seemed to close in, visions of the Earth trapping me, imprisoning me in the rock swamped me. I needed to get *out*. Quick steps took me back to the pinch. I pushed the basket back onto the ledge, squeezing through when the ground began to shake.

*What did I do, what did I do?*

Slow at first, a trickle of shale bounced past me, steadily growing until it was a waterfall of fine shards. I pushed through the pinch, but it was narrower than before, as though the ravine walls had moved. My breath came rapidly; the Earth was going to take me after all.

I coughed as grit and dust caught in my throat, choking. Struggling, I managed to get one arm through, flailing about on the other side for purchase, but there was nothing. My hands tore on the rough surface, and I yelled in frustration. Rock shook around me, pressing, closing in. Tears ran down my face, leaving muddy tracks laced with salt. I didn't want to die here, gasping, reaching into nothingness.

Warm hands closed around mine, yanking, working me free from my prison. I wiggled my hips through, the crush of rock bruising, but I didn't care. I just wanted to be *out.* The hands wrenched on my arm as larger rocks tumbled onto my legs, and in a mad game of tug of war, I was free.

I lay on something warm and soft, chest heaving, glad of the clean air on this side. I blinked at grit that fell past my lashes, into my eyes. Dirt crusted every inch of me, and I wondered if I'd ever feel clean again.

Pushing up on my elbows, I realised the tremors had stopped. The ground was still—silent. A shudder wracked me. I turned around and came nose-to-nose with Nestor. Squeaking, I backed off in a hurry and landed on my rump. An expression I couldn't quite place hesitated on his face for a long moment, his usual smirk replacing it before I had time to process the change in him fully.

"Nothing with you is normal, is it?" He drawled, making a show of dragging his gaze over me. I looked down at the cuts and bruises covering my arms and realised my shirt was very askew. I straightened it up, feeling odd under his stare. Being near him had never been comfortable—and being alone and isolated added to my disquiet. Mind, he had just saved me—without his help, I would never have gotten free.

"Thank you…"

My words trailed off, unsure what else to say as I collected my basket. Smashed shards littered the top, over half shattered beyond use. I picked out the broken pieces, scanning the ground around me, but there was nothing usable nearby. I winced at the thought of the Keeper's faces when I came back with less than they had required.

Straightening up, I found Nestor far too close to me again. This time anger came, compensating from my fear earlier. Clenching my basket to hide shaking hands, I was ready to cuss at him but stopped, mouth agape when he presented me with a handful of well-formed tubes. He casually slipped them into my basket, stepping back with a little bow and gestured up the hill.

"Shall we?"

I nodded numbly, hoisting the baskets onto my back for the steep climb. The weight lessened. I glanced over my shoulder to see Nestor sling one over his back, nodding at me. I returned the gesture and faced forward again, confused by his actions.

Trekking back to the top cost me the rest of my energy, and by the time we were on the grass of my hill again, shaking encompassed my entire body. I sat on the grass, just breathing, thinking over all that had happened in the ravine. No matter how many times I went over it, I couldn't figure out how I had angered the Earth.

Perhaps this was my comeuppance for creating so much, but I'd never experienced Her anger before. I knew there had been a tremor the day I was born—it was one of the reasons no one socialised with me. Some had blamed me; others had blamed my mother.

Tears began anew at the thought of her and Dad. I missed them so much. Everyone else had a family—even Nestor, Jase, and Mal had each other, regardless of whether they got along or not.

I swallowed down the hurt; my sight blurred as Nestor sat beside me. His skin touched mine in a one-armed hug, and though I stiffened, he didn't move, just sat there with me until the tears passed. With a quick squeeze, he stood, taking both baskets.

"I'll take these up for you. Get yourself cleaned up, get some sleep. You'll need it."

I stared after him, watching until his lean frame disappeared past my greenhouse, back to the rest of our community. Then his words collided in my mind. My Bidding was tomorrow. Too tired to face anyone, I trudged back to my greenhouse to do what he had suggested.

I decided I liked this new Nestor.

# CHAPTER SEVEN

The next morning I avoided contact with Jase. If he didn't know I was leaving for my Bidding, then I wouldn't have to deal with his comforting comments on the way to the Hall or have time to miss him, in case my plan went totally tea kettle up and I became the lone occupant of the Vault before lunch. Or Outcast. Either way, I wouldn't be seeing him again. I couldn't deal with knowing I had to say goodbye but take on empty platitudes instead.

Grits from my roll stuck to my tongue, dry and tasteless. I walked up the hill, appreciating every step. I'd put salve made from my medicinal plants on my bruises and grazes before I curled into bed. The skin stretched new and clear; no souvenier of yesterday's exploits remained.

I watched the rainbows flit about, bright and energetic within their confines. If released, would they shoot about the sky or bounce to the ground across the open ground?

It was quiet on the way through the cooking areas. It was too early for the musicians to be around, though I missed the lightness they brought, the conversation that followed them wherever they played.

My feet pressed lightly into the soil beneath the largest tree outside the Hall. Tall and majestic, it dominated the landscape. Again I experienced a shrinking sensation, the feeling I was only a seed in a much larger world.

At the entrance to the Hall, I hesitated, unwilling to face my fate just yet. The morning seemed particularly vibrant—greens and blues at their best, competing with the auroras above. The canopy of the ancient oak that contained the Hall extended far over the Green. An old myth told of people barricading themselves into this old place against each other, when they turned the sky black, back when it used to be a famed building—a cathedral. Now it's original purpose was lost.

We'd kept some of the pretty windows with their strange, forgotten words and long wooden seats. Perfect for when the entire community filed inside to witness a new law passed. Or a judgement. Fortunately, I was not so significant as to entertain the entire community.

Only the Keepers.

I could hear their chatter from behind the pair of wooden buttresses that served as an entrance to the Cathedral, the original doors long gone.

The tree roots formed an arched roof decorated with coloured slices of glass. This section of buttress curved back in on itself, a series of quick turns that obscured the inside of the Cathedral and was thick enough to muffle most sound. If you shouted, the words still came through but greatly reduced. That's what sounded like was happening now—two loud male voices going at it.

"She thinks she can run this place! As though she can Create whenever she feels like it. It's so *frustrating.* As though she thinks she can get away with anything, without repercussion."

*Oops, that would be me.*

"Well, she has the right, doesn't she? That's her job." Nestor—the Keeper with him must be Mal. He wouldn't speak to anyone else that way, surely. But he couldn't be talking about me. I didn't have the right to Create, that's why I was always in trouble. No one did. Curious, I slid just inside the first buttress.

"Doesn't stop her from being irritating."

Nestor's derisive snort was clear. "You can't have everything, Father. You Create Laws. One might think that was enough."

The tree muffled a grumbled reply. I smirked. Good to know Nestor was as irritating to his own family as he was to me.

A cough startled me, and gentle pressure between my shoulder blades nudged me forward. I stepped into the room, glancing back to see the severe face of a Keeper struggling to mask his amusement. He inclined a greying head, resplendent in white robes bright enough to blind.

My fingertips itched, and I brushed at the front of my dress, conscious of dirt still smattering the stained material. I hadn't managed to wash it since my previous Bidding, having tossed it in a heap, happy to let it crumple up. Now I wished I'd straightened it out. I tugged at it self-consciously, adding to the mess on the front. Another poke in my back kept me moving forward. I stepped into the room, dwarfed in the enormous space.

This place held a presence, as though something unseen existed here. The Keepers said it was the Earth, watching over us—or plain just watching us, waiting for us to err and incite its wrath once again. I hated that. Some omnipotent being controlling us, ruling us. I thought of what the Sky People had said about the universe, our place in the solar system. We kept looking inward, trapped in a society of our own making, letting Her rule us with fear. And I wondered if we didn't have it all wrong.

A tall man towered over Nestor in Keepers' robes. They shared the same angular facial structure and mop of dark hair. But where Nestor's flopped greasily over to one side of his face, the elderly man's dark locks were sprinkled with white, giving him a dramatic look. Neither of them looked remotely like Jase.

Twin pairs of onyx eyes stared in my direction. A prod in the centre of my back sent me shuffling across the floor, my shoulders curving around me in protection. Not the best impression. It wasn't how I'd intended to make my entrance. While both men surveyed me with haughty expressions,

Nestor's held an element of amusement. I resisted the urge to poke my tongue out at him. Barely.

As I approached the Keeper and his son, I looked around, searching for anything to distract myself from the rising panic in my wame. Rainbow light filtered through the windows, decorating the floor in a mosaic of colour.

A woman in Keeper's robes I hadn't noticed when I'd entered the Hall sat on a long bench beneath a stained window. The scene depicted a man with long hair in flowing blue and red robes with a glowing circle around his head, holding a ribbon that dangled from his outstretched hands. I wondered who he had been. Bathed in purple light, the Keeper looked up as I passed by her and smiled. Though I had never spoken to her, I felt marginally better she was here.

A cough turned my attention back to my nemesis. Looking between the two men, I was unsure who that was after yesterday. Amusement twinkled in Nestor's eyes. I hated that he was enjoying this—at my cost, as always.

Mal grunted, gesturing impatiently as he paced the length of the Hall. Nestor bowed grandly to me.

I huffed, walking quickly to the dais. His father strode down the aisle between two long rows of bench seats.

Four large chairs sat on the raised stage perpendicular to the lower hall, facing a single bench. I stared at the spot, my chest roiling. I risked a look over my shoulder, ignoring Nestor's gleeful expression—*the world isn't about you*—to the Keeper behind him.

The woman I'd seen beneath the window followed, last in line, leaving me to wonder who the final Keeper would be for my Bidding.

I approached the bench and sat without being asked; the changed layout unsettling me. Mostly it was the anxiety leading up to my Bidding that got me. The rush of adrenaline post interrogation sickened and exhausted me. Jase had often held me, waiting through the shakes that could last for an age.

This time was different.

Sitting on the bench, I had to look up at the Keepers on their thrones. Feeling small appeared to be the order of the day. I let my snarky thoughts have voice in my mind, hoping to keep the fear at bay, hoping none of them slipped past my lips. Now was not the time to become obnoxious or self-righteous.

I settled as best I could, trying to work out what demure should feel like when people began to filter into the Hall. Far too quickly, people occupied every pew. I searched for Jase amongst the crowd but couldn't find him anywhere. Being so tall, he was usually easy to spot. The unease that had been with me all morning returned in force. I regretted eating my roll.

Refusing to think about what this new trial might mean, I again sought distraction. Nestor lounged against his father's chair, which was more ornate than the other Keepers'. At the far end of the row, an empty chair stood. I wondered again who the final Keeper would be, hoping whoever it was would be sufficiently sympathetic to my plight.

I'd hang on to that thought; it would get me through, I promised myself, until I heard three little words that would seal my fate.

"Nestor, sit *down*."

# Chapter Eight

Exuding confidence and elegance, Nestor reclined in his chair as though he were High King, despite his father's belittlement. For a brief moment, I pitied him, thinking back on his kindness in the ravine. Then I remembered what his presence meant on the Council and crumbled a little more inside.

"He's a Keeper, now?"

The words tumbled from my mouth before I could stop them. Nestor smirked at me silkily. His father raised an eyebrow, and I cringed, pre-empting the knockdown I was about to receive. I looked again at Nestor, lounging in his high-backed chair.

*Why couldn't it be Jase?*

I missed my best friend terribly right now. A hand on my shoulder, his presence beside me, would have given me strength, of which I had little at the moment. Then my thoughts drifted to

Nestor—now that we appeared to be on neutral ground, what did that mean for the outcome of my Bidding, and how would it impact my relationship with Jase? I recalled the odd look that had passed between us when he pulled me from the rock, more confused than ever. I was so deep in thought that I missed the Keeper's opening statement.

Most unfortunately, he noticed too.

"..this is your *sixth* Bidding! I don't understand...CHILD! Are you listening to me?"

I cringed inwardly but held my head high. Bother if I was going to let him see me falter.

"Yes."

"Yes, *what?*"

I sat silent, knowing it would provoke him. I could hear Jase's voice whispering in my head but refused to listen. I was so tired of trying to abide by rules that made no sense, especially in light of what the Sky People had revealed of the knowledge hidden within the Library, and of their nature, their ability to Create. Again, thanks to Jase. I had to remember to ask about the Library. He seemed to know so much about our community—our people—that I didn't, but I knew that separation was partly my choice, too.

"Veritas, you had your final warning in these very chambers not a day ago. To see you here again, so soon, shows you have no remorse for your actions."

The Keeper droned on, and I struggled to keep up with him, chest tight, scanning the crowd for Jase, spotting him at the back leaning against a white wall. I wished he was closer. I took a few quick breaths to wake myself up. Mal stared at me for a moment as though assessing whether I would pass out and continued.

"Therefore, we sentence you to the Vault, where you will reconsider your actions at our...convenience."

Wait; what? Where was the chance for me to defend myself? A commotion broke out in the crowd—some whistles and cheers but mostly angry voices. It was good to know they were as shocked as me. I shot upright in my seat, mouth open ready to fight, but a tiny movement distracted me. Nestor sat looking hard at his father, a frown creasing those angular features. His hand, hidden behind a swath of material from his coat, made a downward waving gesture in my direction.

My mouth snapped shut. I had never trusted Nestor before, but perhaps it was the way he looked at his father that gave me pause. I glanced around at the other two Keepers. They just watched Mal with calm, almost vacant expressions, and it hit me that they were expecting this. My sentence was preordained. They'd fixed this before I'd even entered the Hall. The ball of roiling worms was back in my stomach. I jumped as Nestor cleared his throat.

"Father, perhaps such a sentence is harsh— Veritas has not yet had the chance to rectify her mistake of yesterday."

Nestor kept his gaze solid on his father. What game was he playing? I still didn't trust the change in him.

"You are not yet elected on this Council and are here in an observatory capacity only."

The Keeper dismissed his son. Nestor's nose crinkled, and I wondered again at his motives.

"You are decided on this course of action?"

Father and son locked eyes in a battle of wills. I sat frozen, confused. My heart pounded, cool sweat prickling my skin. I desperately wanted to scratch it away but didn't dare move. Finally, his father spoke.

"I am resolved."

"Then, I withdraw my accusation."

The two Keepers sucked in a breath at the same time, and I felt the air drain from the room. Nestor's father sat as frozen as I as his son continued.

"I must have been incorrect. I am certain if you visit the Ark now, you will find any lack of evidence worthy of such a...*harsh* sentence."

A small sigh escaped me. They had planned this together then—he and Jase. Mal swivelled my way too fast for me to remove the confusion from my face. Triumph lit his eyes, and I cursed inwardly.

I caught Nestor's slightly panicked expression before it returned to its usual cold marble fascade. He faced his father. The Keeper's face was swollen, tight with a slow-burning rage.

"You," he pointed a smooth finger at me, "will follow me to the Vault. You," a backward gesture to his younger son as he turned his back, "are dismissed."

Cries erupted, filling the Hall, but I ignored them all. Nestor's eyes held mine for a moment, and I tried to convey my gratitude without giving anything away to the rest of the room. He had shown his hand—and I still didn't understand why—to his father, before the other Keepers, before the entire community. There would be no white robe for him now, despite his parentage.

As Keepers were a heritage-based position, Mal's line would end here. Jase had told his father in no uncertain terms he would never wear the white robes many years ago before he came of age. I'd always wondered how Mal had taken that—if his face had been as bloated and red then as it was now. Jase had told me about it afterward, and I had laughed with him beneath the night auroras.

It only occurred to me now to question how he had felt about going against his father's wishes so drastically. Though he had shown me the freedom it gave him, for him to Create as he would—jealousy twinged me—I had never questioned the pain it caused him to go against family. As I didn't have one, I often ignored the concept of filial piety.

Nestor broke our gaze first with a sharp, upward jut of his chin in my direction. He turned in a swirl of black, stepping down from the dais without bowing. I stared at Mal's retreating back, white robes brushing the flagstone flooring from another era. I didn't want to follow him. Questions muddled my mind, but I got to ask none of them. The serene Keeper approached me, her hand gentle on my elbow, turning me to follow Mal into the bowels of the Hall. She gave me a reassuring nod and pressed me forward.

My feet followed the Keeper's robes automatically, one before the other as panic consumed me. I had no chance to defend myself, no control over my fate—something I'd always prided myself on.

*You did this to yourself.*

I closed my eyes and left the main room of the Hall.

# Chapter Nine

They didn't need to touch me, to drag me away, though hands reached out to grasp my dress. I stood tall, capable of dealing with my punishment under my own steam. If I weren't able to control my fate, I'd at least have a measure over how I entered it.

I followed Mal to a side door I hadn't been down to before. A pair of small rooms with chairs and a tatty, red curtain lined the side of the corridor. A screen of interwoven wood separated them in a partition. It wasn't the work of our weavers, with their baskets of chunky roots or fine flax bags. This was a relic from before the Last Storm. Neither room had a door, and I wondered at their purpose.

I glanced over my shoulder, searching for— hope? A saviour? No, I would deal with this on my own. Nestor sent his usual amused smirk my way, and I wished I hadn't looked back. Apparently, he had recovered from his moment of conscience. Movement caught my eye as I turned, and I looked back again, staring past Nestor this time.

Jase stood beneath an archway, unusually pasty. I sent him a broad grin that I didn't feel and waved. Nestor frowned, needlessly wondering why I was waving at him. I picked a jaunty pace, happy to add to his confusion, and followed their father into the depths of the Hall.

Out of their sight behind a heavy column, my faux confidence crumbled in the dim light of the hallway, the sense of presence—peace—removed as I followed the Keeper into the bowels of the Earth. Broad sandstone bricks became packed soil, trailing roots of the great Figtree above. I shivered, not liking the odour or the enclosed space. The walls pressed in. I rubbed my arms; sure I was already covered in dirt, entombed beneath the place that had housed my final Bidding. I tripped on a root, sprawling on the floor in a self-fulfilling prophecy. The Keeper's footsteps echoed dully in the tunnel, never stopping.

"Keep up."

He didn't turn, and I wondered why there wasn't

someone behind me to keep me going. What if I ran, made my escape? Perhaps it had never happened before. But where would I go? The rest of the Keepers were likely still in the Hall, and though Nestor had stretched his neck out for me this once, I doubted he would be amused if I sprinted back to him, clutching his robes, begging for help.

That gave me a giggle. Mal checked over his shoulder. Probably thought I was having hysterics. I snickered again, my mind wandering. Nestor's intervention still confused me. I contemplated his motives as I scrambled to my hands and knees, shunting myself forward, slow in the loose dirt I'd kicked up.

Desperate not to lose the light Mal carried, I sprinted to catch up and almost ran into him as he stopped abruptly. My hands were outstretched, just shy of touching his pristine robes. I smothered a giggle, the image of him with two dusty handprints square in the centre of all that whiteness in my mind. Would the other Keepers be amused? Did they even laugh?

I held myself back as we reached the end of the hallway. A jangle of metal—so rare—and a click bounced around the blunt tunnel. An ominous creak announced our arrival at the Vault. The great door was black, stained—or burnt; I couldn't tell in the dimness. It melded into the wall surrounding it. Mal's hand was stark in contrast, pushing it open.

Rooted to the spot, I peered into the darkness. Whatever existed beyond the hallway was hidden in blackness so thick, Mal's poor light couldn't penetrate it. He motioned me forward, a sneer marring an otherwise cranky face. I just stared into the gloom, unmoving. Not a shaft of light or air moved. I blinked, mouth dry, eyes itching. My tongue stuck to the roof of my mouth, and I pried it free, wondering if I'd inadvertently swallowed a clump of earth.

Mal gestured again with his light, then sighed impatiently.

"Is there–," I stuttered, lips not working properly. I swallowed and tried again. "Is there anyone else in there?"

Mal sighed again, and with a sharp movement, he swept his free arm up into the darkness. I tracked its movement until it disappeared into the gloom, confused. A sharp shove sent me stumbling into the darkness, realisation dawning far too late. I flailed, grasping for anything I could, fingers brushing soft material as I passed by Mal. I missed the doorway and slammed into the darkness. The light disappeared in a soft thud as the Keeper sealed me into the Vault.

Despite the fear that bloomed in my chest, I smiled into the dark, knowing I'd slapped a dirt coated hand to the front of his robes.

I hit the floor and inhaled dead earth. It didn't taste like the dirt in my greenhouse that sometimes got into my mouth when a particularly vivacious plant demonstrated its independence. This earth had the taste of death.

I crumbled a little more inside at the thought of my Creations. Had Jase and Nestor stripped my greenhouse, killing what I'd given life—intelligence—to? My eyes closed, and for a moment, I forgot the darkness, recalling the rainbow light filtering through the greenery, warm beneath the glass Jase had placed just for me, so I had somewhere safe to live.

My mind flashed with white light, a day beneath the frozen auroras. The touch of my plants—my last

Creation, curling around my wrists, tracing the lines of dirt pressed into my palms, the scent of heady, dark earth. I breathed it in—and choked, falling back to the present. Death clotted in my throat. I coughed, clawing the floor, and the urge to escape returned to me in force.

I lumbered to the door, half bent over and retching, arms blindly outstretched. More steps, too many. I stumbled on, past where I thought the door should be. Lost in the darkness, I felt small, insignificant in an unknown place.

My feet tumbled over each other as I turned in a circle, dizzy. Where was the door? Where were the walls? I couldn't find *anything*. I raced in a line, sure to hit something, but found nothing. How big was this place? I coughed again, sucking in air that seemed devoid of oxygen. Fresh air eluded me. I swivelled, walking backwards. My mind wandered, terrified in the dark. Where was everything? I couldn't breathe, couldn't feel anything but the floor.

I tripped again, backwards this time, and fell— farther than where the floor should be. I reached up senselessly—there was nothing there to save me as

I descended into blackness.

Sharp stone bent me backwards, my spine protesting as my feet shot over my head, and I somersaulted down a flight of stairs, my face smacking the steps. I crumpled in a heap at the bottom, resting my cheek on the rough stone. Tears tracked down my cheeks. I knew I was a mess, and glad Jase wasn't here to see me like this.

*Jase.*

The tears came faster. I missed him so much— just glimpsing his face as I'd left the Hall had almost undone me. I wanted those strong arms around me, shielding me as he always had. No matter how I strived for independence, proud to be strong, and stand up on my own, I knew he was always there to stop me falling when I leapt.

But he wasn't here now. Wetness pooled at my neck, dampening the material of my dress. Not so white now, I was sure. I shifted, trying to sit. Pain screamed in my arms, across my shoulder, down my back. I gasped, light sparking across my vision. I knew it was in my eyes, but for a single moment, I took comfort in its presence. Then my world was black again, and all I knew was pain.

I woke to the same darkness as before, but this time it was less frightening. Everything ached, and my head spun. For a moment, I wondered if the Keepers had sent me here to die. But surely even they wouldn't be so cruel. Pressing into the cold stone with filthy hands, I hauled my aching self into a sitting position, taking stock of my injuries. It appeared I'd come through my tumble relatively unscathed. Bruises abound, but apart from my tears, I couldn't feel anything wet and assumed I wasn't bleeding.

Plenty of areas were tender—I'd be a rainbow of colour if ever I got back to the light, rather like Mal with his dirty robes. A smile tickled the corners of my lips, and I started to giggle. Laughter bubbled up, and I squawked, grasping at my sides until they ached. Bending over, I gasped for air, but the giggles wouldn't stop. I snorted, and the giggles turned to coughs, tears welling for a new reason. Eventually, I was silent.

Tightness began in my chest as I stared, squeezed by the blackness. No shadows to scare me, as everything was one. I stretched my fingers on my lap, feeling they were there, determined not to lose myself to the madness that already brushed the edges of my consciousness. Movement kept me calm, rolling my wrists, swinging sore arms, rotating my shoulders and neck, knowing I was there. I clenched my stomach, pressing my legs together, arching my feet, spreading my toes out. I was here. All here.

So out of control of the situation, I needed to hold onto the only thing I was sure of anymore. Knowing I had life still in me, determined not to let the loss of light—of fresh air—beat me. I closed my eyes—they were useless anyway—and listened. My breath slid out, and I sat silent, hollow chested.

Nothing. Nothing moved. Not the buzz of an insect or the slither of something...unknown in the dark. I drew in a long, slow breath and felt around. The stairs I'd crashed down were cool, rough stone, the floor hard-packed earth. The smell of death was less prevalent here—more of wood, combined with a deep, berry smell. *Fruit.* I smiled, pleased to have identified something of my surroundings.

It made the dark less frightening, less unknown, somehow. I began to stand, wincing at the soreness of my ankles. My right leg felt tight, swollen, reminding me of Mal's back in the Hall.

I grinned, suddenly revelling in the pain. Now I knew I was alive. I'd survive the Vault, no matter what the Keepers' intent. Whatever they believed it would do to me. They held the secret of the Vault over us like a rope around our necks, but I refused to let it conquer me.

Tentative steps took me forward, in just one direction this time. I tried to make my steps as natural in length as I could, despite the pain, counting as I went. It wasn't far this time until I hit something. My hands closed around sharp edges, pressing my nose right up to the object and breathed. *Wood*. I ran my hands down and along tracing the contours, the roughness of each surface. *Wooden shelves*.

They had to be over three hundred years old, which probably made them pretty rickety. I made a note not to lean on them. After the Last Storm, there hadn't been a chance for people to make anything new. Between the calamity of the storm and the aftermath of the Earth's rage, humanity was too busy surviving.

My touch was gentle; I didn't want the planks disintegrating over me when I couldn't see to save myself. Who knew what might topple down on top of me if I started digging around. I really didn't need any further injuries. I traced the rack upwards—it stretched high,  taller than my hands could reach. I returned to the shelf in front of me. Rounded shapes lined the shelf in either direction.

In one direction, the wall was twenty-two steps. I returned to centre—only nine steps to the other side. I must be in some kind of cellar or chamber beneath the Hall. This room seemed so much smaller than the one I'd lost myself in at the top of the stone stairs.

I fiddled around with the objects on the shelf, amusing myself with guessing what they were to pass the time. I idly wondered how long I would be staying down here in the dark. Now that I had pulled myself together somewhat, it wasn't as frightening. It was just a large, empty space, and I was alone in it.

I found a short, stubby handle at the base of one of the barrels. I twiddled with it and got wet. Swearing, I fiddled with it until the flow ceased.

Rich, fruity notes hung in the air, saturating my skin and clothes. Blasted tap—then I realised how thirsty I was and bent down for a drink.

The fluid that filled my mouth wasn't water—though it explained the berry smell that saturated the dry air down here. I swallowed more of the juice, craving anything to wash the taste of dirt and blood from my mouth. I swished some around and spat it onto the floor. So much better. Fumbling about to find the barrel again, my hand knocked into something loose. It landed right on my foot, so I was able to collect it with ease in the dark, leaving one hand on the shelf, so I didn't lose that, too.

The small object turned out to be a cup—wooden, not a glass relic thankfully. That would have smashed and made a mess. I decided not to give myself any more injuries.

The little cup filled quickly, overflowing only a little. Dizzying aromas permeated the small area. I slid down the shelving to the floor, managing not to land in the puddle I'd created. I gave a little giggle—*created*. It seemed funny, now.

Still giggling, I downed the rest of the cup and reached up to refill it, trying to catch the overflow in my mouth underneath. Sweet juice splashed my face, dampening my dress. It was cool and sticky, like being beneath a waterfall. That hit me as humorous. I giggled again, sipping from the cup more slowly.

Tiredness swarmed over me, my head drooping. Thoughts of my greenhouse swirled behind closed eyes; all my Creations—from my first sentient vine of many years past to the glowing mini-suns of yesterday. She was such a cheeky plant. I fondly recalled the way the little suns peeked over my shoulder when I was working—almost like eyes, checking what I was doing.

Any sudden movement and they shot into hiding along the roof, leaving me in filtered darkness. But she seemed to know I liked the light and warmth it provided, as the suns always came back.

The images changed to Jase, weaving the vines together as he made my greenhouse for me, so many years ago. It made me grumpy that he got to Create when I found myself incarcerated the same thing. I hefted the tiny cup, letting it slid to the tips of my fingers and hurled it as hard as I could. A clang told me that it hit the wall opposite.

Regret soured me almost immediately—now what was I going to use for drinking? My tongue craved the juice. I bent back, flicking on the tap again, glad when the fluid trickled straight into my mouth. I swallowed until I was full, and my mouth overflowed, just as the cup had. I turned the tap off again and resumed daydreaming about Jase.

Those strong arms—I loved the muscles in his forearms. I could stare at those all day. I loved watching him work, loved the way he consoled me. How safe I felt with him. As though he were a sun, and I revolved around him. I smiled at the idea of Jase being a star—a sun—giving warmth and light to our people.

Part of me wished he had taken the mantle as a Keeper, someone strong and true to lead our small community. There was no ego about him, and we desperately needed Keepers we could trust, that didn't lord their menial power over others. Then I remembered why I was here in the first place, breaking the few rules we had—and realised if he had, we could never be friends. My dreams would be all I had, with no hope beneath them.

Brightness shone through my closed eyelids, and

I flickered them open. I blinked in the sudden glare, searching for the source. Tiny suns clustered against the ceiling, bobbing merrily. Warmth radiated from my palm.

I stared down at the little sun sitting right in my hand. I bounced it a little, and it floated, joining its kin. My hand warmed again, and I gasped as a small light budded in the centre of my palm, rising until it, too, was a tiny, glowing ball of light. I waved to it and could swear I heard it jingle at me in response.

My fingers trailed through the bobbing lights. They bounced into one another, pinging against the ceiling as they chattered in a jingling language. I looked around the room, seeing my prison properly for the first time.

Row upon row of barrels filled shelving to the ceiling. Though it wasn't a large room, that was still a lot of barrels. I stumbled over to the cup I'd thrown earlier and placed it back onto one of the shelves, swaying a little. Fresh air would be good right now, though that was far from likely. But the lights gave me a distraction—explore.

Tall cupboards lined one end of the room. Curious, I lifted one of the metal handles, studying its curved surface, smooth with the use of years long gone. It creaked, stiff, the edges around the keyhole encrusted with the rust. I pushed again, and the old door caved in a little, giving me room to pry it open.

The light didn't extend to the depths of the cupboard. I collected a handful of lights, releasing them inside. They bobbed to the roof, illuminating the contents. Reflections shone back at me from swords and weapons dulled with age and patchy with rust. Some sections of the armoury still held the shine of their former glory.

Making weapons of any kind was forbidden—not only was there a law against violence of any kind, after we'd lost so many since the Last Storm—stealing the Earth's resources was against our laws. Fear of Her power kept us from mining natural deposits.

I reached in, hesitating, then grasped the edge of a long object. Not expecting the weight, it almost slipped from my grasp, jammed beneath an assortment of killing tools that had fallen from their allocated places. I jiggled it, pushing against the cupboard with my knees. The thing finally shot free.

I overbalanced, landing on my backside.

The stone floor was cold against my back as I lay stuck beneath my bounty. It took me a few rolls before I was able to regain my feet, panting a little. Squatting down, I rubbed the broad surface, scraping away rust where it had oxidised in the little air left down here. Pictures emerged, a tall, spiked animal, twice the size of the man beside it, depicted bearing the object up between himself and the beast.

A word dredged itself from my lessons on history, stories told to young children of the great dinosaurs that once roamed the earth, men conquering them. That was it—a shield, for protection. It contrasted bleakly against our history of killing and death, the stories of great men. Pity, there were few about women that had survived.

Disgruntled, I tried to lift the shield and toppled over, taking more skin off on the flagstones as I rolled head over teakettle. I lay there, giggling as the room swirled around me. My lights became a blur, and I closed my eyes. Water. I needed water. I squeezed my eyes tighter, taking in deep breaths.

My eyelashes stuck together. Grit fell into my

eyes as I struggled to open them. Rubbing them was a mistake. I sat up, the room still swaying. How long had I been asleep? I crawled to the steps, mouth parched. Unless the Keepers were intent on actually killing me—no violence rule my butt—they would have left some form of sustenance in the room.

Wouldn't they? My head was fuzzy. My thoughts dashed from one thing to another, what I'd been searching for a moment ago fading quickly. I couldn't seem to keep a thought straight. And I couldn't see. Confused, I inched up the steps into the room above, peering into the dimness. Irritated I was unable to see farther than my own hand, I waved at the lights, and they swarmed overhead, brightening the large space.

It wasn't as cavernous as I had initially thought. My footprints clearly outlined where I had entered the room. A scuffed patch showed where I had fallen when Mal shoved me inside. More footprints travelled deeper into the Vault, twisting and turning back on themselves as I had lost myself in the darkness, leading to the stairs.

I swayed to my feet. The air was different here— I recalled the taste of death in my mouth, stomach clenching. I swallowed, searching for a distraction, but this thought stayed with me. The smell seemed to come from the dirt floor, different from the flagstones of the lower room. Here, shelves lined the walls, deep cuts into the rock strata. Cotton fabric lay in a few of them, so old it disintegrated at my softest touch.

I trailed my fingers along the cuts in the rock, dust trickling from them in a steady stream. The lights came too, following me. I waved them forward of me, lighting a long passage. Some way down, three tunnels forked off, each leading in a different direction. How far did they go beneath the Hall? The rows cut into the rock were smoother here, as though many hands had run over this area. Wondering what was so significant about them, I selected the centre one that seemed to delve deepest into the bowels of the Hall. The corridor was long—and more tunnels split off from it.

My hand hit the ledge beside me, shunting its contents into the air. An old, bony skull stared into my face, and I yelped, scrambling backward out of the tunnel. I fell face-first into the dirt of the main room, tasting death. Again. A thought niggled me. I tried to pin it down, but images and thoughts flitted around: what I imagined the Last Storm to look like, the monsters men became afterward, ripping each other apart.

So many had hidden themselves away, tiny units scattered about the cities. Larger buildings had housed what remained of cities—I couldn't grasp the idea of only buildings and no forests. People had survived inside as long as they could, leaving when they thought it was safe. Then She attacked, and people went back into hiding, better provisioned than before.

Generations passed in fear, leading to who we were today. The realisation of what the ledges were for—and who occupied them—hit me. I lay there in the dirt, shivering.

What if I had wandered down one of the tunnels, gotten turned around, and lost? Not such a stretch for a *vapid-minded klutz* like me. I might never have been able to return to the main room. Would I have become just another set of bones in clothes, like those on the shelves?

My skin prickled, wondering if I, too, would have lain on a piece of unoccupied rock. The material nearest the entrance to the Vault was newest, though still ancient to me. How many had the Keepers sent here to die? I swallowed back the urge to vomit. My lights clustered around me, snuggling. I collected a great armful, resting on them. I didn't feel quite so alone, but the horrors of this chamber illuminated the Keepers for me in a new way.

I knew it wasn't often people were sent to the Vault—well, as far as I knew. I resolved to ask Jase about it—or perhaps Nestor, seeing as we were in unusual territory now. It seemed the sort of thing he would take pleasure in knowing—the sordid details.

I shifted my legs, untangling them from the material that had accompanied me on my tunnel adventure. The skull with its toothless, gaping maw tumbled onto my lap, and I gave a little shriek.

*Pull it together, V. It's a dead bit of bone.*

I hiccupped again, reaching for the skull, fingers paused inches from the bone. When I touched it, the bone was cool. I brought it to eye level, wondering who it had belonged to, which age and terrors he had survived—or not. I swayed where I sat.

That's how the boys found me when they arrived

to rescue me—eye-to-eye, grinning at the morbid skull, surrounded by a bunch of glowing lights.

# Chapter Ten

The heavy door slammed open, dangling half off its hinges. Jase stood in the doorway, chest heaving with exertion. Nestor slid past him, a bemused expression decorating his face as he stared down at me. I smiled giddily, waving the skull in greeting.

The boys gaped at me in my puddle of rotted cloth and remains. Suns jingled about me, merry in their chatter. As the boys edged further into the room, they clustered tightly about me. It felt like overprotection, and suddenly, their heat was too much. I shot to my feet, swaying.

'Whoa," Jase grabbed my arm, steadying me. But though I was still, the room wasn't. Nestor grasped my other arm with cold fingers. Everything I'd drunk rose to my lips in spectacular fashion. Both boys swore, leaping out of the way. Jase dragged me back to avoid the splatter.

"She's drunk," Nestor hissed.

Jase growled at him, the sound reverberating in his chest. I looked up at him with a silly grin and bleary eyes. A small smiled etched the corners of his mouth as he observed his brother.

"You'd know. I remember you crawling up the hallway when you got into Dad's aloe wine."

"Mmm. I thought a giant spider was hanging above me. I recall *you* crawling with me back to my room."

"Well, you wouldn't come with me otherwise."

The boys laughed over my head.

I sighed softly, glad to see them get along for once. My movement attracted Jase's attention. His gaze swept up and down my body; his expression mirroring Nestor's when he had entered the Vault. My eyes followed his, and I gave a little gasp in understanding, my appearance appalling even me.

Weeping cuts and bruises smeared with dirt decorated my arms and legs. My once-white dress was stained red with dribbled patches, dusted with the remains of whoever I had pulled from the rock ledges. I giggled at the thought, leaning into Jase.

"We need to get you cleaned up," he murmured,

inspecting my face. Even with a gentle touch, I winced at each spot he probed.

"Water," I croaked.

Nestor reached back without looking to retrieve a jug, which he poured liberally over my head. I squawked under the icy deluge, glaring at him. Still the same smart ass he'd always been. He smirked.

"Much better."

Jase shoved him out of the way, towing me to the door.

"We have to get you out of here."

I nodded, swiping dripping stands hair from my face. Tiredness washed over me, and I dragged my feet towards the door.

"Come on."

Jase tugged my arm again, but I just looked at him.

"We have to go," he insisted again.

I nodded wearily, following him past Nestor, who gestured behind me.

"Are your friends coming too?"

I looked back at the lights, now clustered together, bobbing hopefully. I had a thought, pulling my arm from Jase's grasp. Snaring a pair of suns, I pressed them together, melding them. As I'd predicted, they sank seamlessly into one another. I continued with the rest, gathering a large ball in my hand.

As the last of the light disappeared into it, I pressed both hands to the globe, shrinking it down until it was back to the size of the one I'd formed in my palm. Bright and slightly warmer, but manageable. I twisted my hand, letting it spin across my skin. The boys watched, mesmerised. I bounced it once and flicked it to Nestor, hitting him in the face. He caught the orb in one hand, rubbing his nose with his closed fist.

"All yours." I sang softly, leading them out the door. In the corridor, I stopped, unsure. Jase brushed past me, his hand warm on my icy skin. He headed back through the tunnel to the empty Hall. Devoid of people, our footsteps echoed, mocking our escape. Once again, the sense of presence filled me. Peace settled on me, and for a moment, I understood why people would have come here in times of turmoil.

I stopped near the dais, where an old wooden bench stood. I laid a hand on it and closed my eyes, ignoring the whispers and hisses from the boys.

I could have wandered forever in those tunnels, I realised with abrupt clarity. Wandered until my feet couldn't take another step; until my mouth was dry.

Until I was the death in the earth.

"Thank you," I whispered—to what, to whom, I wasn't sure.

I opened my eyes and turned back to the boys who studied me. One pale-skinned and sallow with dark eyes that missed nothing, the other lean muscled and tanned with that piercing blue gaze I'd dreamt about—bright, like the sun. I smiled, reaching out to Jase, who took my hand despite the dirt and grime, careful of my injuries.

Nestor rolled his eyes, muttering something about birds in love. I shushed him, sliding between the buttress roots of the great arched doorway. I stared into the shadows with new light, seeing how the roots of the giant tree held up a crumbling building centuries old. The bark was thick and rough beneath my fingers. I marvelled at its age and the enormous task it took on, never bowing under its weight.

Under the frozen sky, I stopped and took a deep breath, clearing my lungs of the dead earth and fruity smell of the Vault, glad the nausea passed. If I never encountered berries again, it would be too soon.

Nestor gripped my elbow. I looked down in surprise at his cool fingers. When had we been on speaking terms, let alone touching? I let the boys draw me into the shadows of the tree line. Jase headed for our favourite rock, where we often shared our evening meal.

I hesitated, not wanting to introduce Nestor to a place that was special to me. That meal with my best friend gave me peace as rainbows became auroras in the evening sky. I didn't want Nestor intruding on that. Regardless of his recent change, he still felt like an outsider to me.

Jase motioned me forward, disappearing behind a screen of trees. Nestor was still smirking at me. He even winked. I started, then looked down to see what he saw. My white—albeit stained—dress was practically see-through, thanks to the water he'd thrown at me. I drew myself up to my full height, nearly reaching his shoulder, armed with my hardest glare. I stepped sharply into him, and he had the grace to look surprised.

"I saw what you did in the Vault," I hissed under my breath, just loud enough for him to hear. His head canted to the side.

"Besides your newest Creations?" he quizzed, wriggling fingers in the pocket he had secreted my ball of suns. I wasn't about to let him draw me in with a sleight of hand distraction.

"The water."

He just smirked, and I quelled the urge to wipe it from his face. My fingers twitched. I kept my hands firmly pressed to my sides.

"You knew the jug was there. You didn't even have to look to where it was. You'd been in there before."

His eyes darkened beneath my accusations.

"Perhaps I put it there, setting the room up for you, as it were. You know your sentence was preordained," Nestor added.

I did know. It had been plain to me at the end that this last Bidding was nothing more than a show pony for the Keeper's own ends.

"When were you in there?" I demanded, refusing

to take the bait Nestor offered. "Is it somewhere you go for a nap? You do look like you could do with a little light."

He grabbed my arm before I could move away.

"You have no idea what you're talking about," he growled, pivoting me on the spot and shoving me in the direction Jase had taken.

I stumbled around the trees, catching my hand on the rock. Jase steadied me with a grin—unaware anything was amiss. I closed my eyes for a moment as he wrapped a long shawl around me. His arms followed, and I rested my head on his hard chest, listening to the steady beat of his heart. So many questions ran around my head. I squeezed my eyes closed, determined to shut out all the chatter, all the questions, and enjoy his warmth.

He pulled me down onto the rock, arms still wrapped around me. I winced a little as he bumped my bruises but didn't move away, not wanting to break contact. Nestor passed me food that I took with a resentful glare and fell upon it like a woman starved.

I was just full of contradictions today. Or maybe always.

Jase's finger's trailed through my hair as I ate, gently detangling the wild mess it had become. I nudged him away, not rebuking, but I wanted to keep the food to myself. I twisted to grin at him as I swallowed, choking a little on a chunk of dry bread. He passed me water with a grin. I gulped it down, watching Nestor over the rim of the cup. He held my gaze—I wasn't sure if it was in defiance or amusement. Finally, I tore my eyes back to Jase.

"How did you get me out?"

Jase nodded to Nestor, who shrugged.

"I waited until my father came back, cursing. Something about "defiled robes" and "harlot of hell," he grinned at me, and I looked down.

Yep, that was me. Just add these great titles to my repertoire. Nestor continued. "He left the floor in a dither—I hailed brother dear here into the Hall and dragged you back out. Though it was more...eventful...than I imagined."

I glanced at Jase through my lashes, ready to hide if he held anger or disdain at the way I'd treated his father, coward that I was. Instead, his eyes were intense, staring down at me. I barely dared reach out to him.

"Thank you. *Both* of you," I switched my glance between the two, day and night. "I could have *died* down there without you."

Jase crouched in front of me, grasping my hands. His warmth penetrated my icy skin.

"I would have found you—no matter what it took." Nestor kicked dirt at us, but Jase's gaze never wavered. "No matter what it took."

I leaned into him, wishing we were alone.

"Thank you," I whispered again, just for one person.

I looked up at Nestor, still puzzling over his actions in the Hall.

"And thank *you*...though I'm not sure what for yet. For what you said at my Bidding. To your father."

Jase winced, but Nestor's gaze held mine. He nodded, still for a moment before disappearing into the tree line.

"Let's look at you." Jase pulled me into the light running his fingers down my arms, raising pebbled flesh wherever he touched.

I shivered, and he glanced at me with a half-grin, continuing down to my ankles. Lifting the hem of my stained dress slightly, he gasped at the bruises, gently pressing around each one to acknowledge them. His fingers ran up the insides of my calves to my knees, where they rested, squeezing gently.

"Hurt?" he murmured.

I shook my head, unable to speak. His fingers stroked the back of my knees, reaching up to my thighs. Quivers shot to my core. I leaned down to him. A cough interrupted us.

We both turned to see the female Keeper, splendid in her unstained robes. I tugged the shawl tighter as Jase's fingers disappeared, squeezing my ankles quickly on their way down.

"When you're ready, I have your new sentence." She left as abruptly as she arrived, stepping from the rock ledge with a grace I could never hope to achieve. She looked over her shoulder, catching my eye. "To the Library."

The Library. In my panic, I had forgotten all about it. We followed the Keeper down the hill, meeting Nestor halfway there. Jase slipped his arm around my waist as we passed his brother, pulling me close. I closed my eyes, not wanting to see his smirk again, grateful for the protection from the world Jase offered.

I ducked my head into his shoulder, wondering if they would take me directly to the Library, then realised we were going the wrong way. Excitement blossomed in my chest—how could I hide that my new sentence was the very place I'd wanted to visit? I wondered how it had come about and resolved to ask the Keeper as soon as I had the chance.

She led us back to my greenhouse.

"Take the time to change, wash up a little, enjoy the night with your friends." She stressed the last word a little. I stopped, considering. Nestor had just broken me out of what little prison we had. He had saved my life yesterday.

But I still had questions for him.

The boys waited outside while I washed and put on fresh clothing. I looked longingly at my bed, wishing I could tumble into it. Instead, I made a quick thermos of tea, a blend I made from aromatic leaves my Creations provided. Filled to the brim, it would be enough for us all. No waste was allowed in our community, a hang-up perhaps from days long gone, but it stayed with us. Everything had a purpose—or two or three. Throwing a satchel with the thermos and the wrap Jase had provided over my shoulders, I re-joined the boys outside. The air was chilly as we tackled the hill for evening fare, and I was glad of the warmth of the wrap.

At the top of the hill, the Green housed the main community work area—the glass ovens off to the far side of the area, cooking stations beside it, keeping all the heat in one area. Artists and musicians played in the centre whilst weavers used their rhythms to complete their own work.

The boys flanked my sides, fending off questions and dark looks by their presence alone. When did we become a unit? I thought of how many laws they had broken in helping me escape and were glad they were Keepers' sons; maybe they would stay out of the trouble I caused. The thought gave me pause and filled me with regret.

"I'm sorry," I murmured, keeping my head down. I had never been good at apologies.

"For what?"

I glanced over at Nestor.

"For, well, dragging you into my troubles. I've lost you your job," I mumbled.

Both boys laughed, and I looked between them, loving they were getting along but hating that I was left out. They stopped when they saw my consternation. Jase slipped an arm around my shoulders. I leaned into him, looking up expectantly, but it was Nestor who broke the silence.

"He didn't want it any more than I did."

I mulled that over, thinking of Mal's temper, how he treated Nestor in public. The pity I'd felt in the Hall returned.

"What do you want to do?"

It was the first time I'd asked. Our relationship was so abrasive; personal preferences had never come into it. I studied the tall, isolated boy who had become a lean, quiet man. When had that happened? His expression changed minutely, brows tilted, shoulders down. Almost as tall as Jase, he stood a head above me with little of his brother's natural bulk. Long, tapered fingers carried scrapes from our adventures in the ravine yesterday.

I realised with a start that I hadn't told Jase about it. As though reading my mind, a tiny shake of Nestor's head warned me not to. I trusted him enough now to hold my tongue, though I was sure I would speak to Jase about it sometime later. Angular planes framed his face as shadows dipped around us. The evening brightened as the auroras performed their dance in the darkened skyscape above us.

"I like," Nestor stopped, cleared his throat, and tried again. "I like music. Flute, pipes." He shrugged, turning away as though embarrassed. Words tumbled from my lips before I fully formed the thought.

"Does your father know?"

By the tightening of Jase's shoulders, I gathered he did. Nestor occupied himself with spooning soup into my bowl, passing it back to me, and filling his brother's. The server waved to Jase, avoiding my smile. I breathed deeply, wishing I was back in my Ark.

"Dad hates it." Jase's words came out as a soft hiss, staring hard at Nestor's back.

The smell of the stew almost undid me. The small bowl of food the boys had provided me seemed long ago. I pressed my forehead against Jase's shoulder, gently nudging for more information. His mouth set in a hard line.

"He– Dad tossed our instruments into the ravine years ago. I stopped playing, found a new way to occupy myself," he looked ruefully at his hands, and I remembered the ease with which he had taken up Twinning. "Nestor didn't give up so easily. He still plays with the musicians. They lend him their instruments, out of Ma– out of the Keeper's sights. In case someone reports back to Dad."

A bowl appeared beneath his nose, and Jase took it, nodding his thanks. Another found its way into my hands. We headed toward the rock Jase and I usually shared. As we entered the edge of the tree line, the chatter died around us, foliage dampening the noise. It didn't feel so alien to have Nestor with us this time.

Jase and I settled on the rock. Nestor planted himself at our feet, looking out over the precipice. Trees enclosed us on all sides, shadows merging in the dying light.

We ate in comfortable silence, wooden spoons clanking dully on dried clay bowls. Jase produced rolls halfway through. I raised an eyebrow. Had he stolen them? Most likely, he'd sweet-talked one of the middle-aged baker women who doted on him, sons a rarity between them.

Twilight was fully upon us when Nestor collected our bowls. He departed with a quick wave, an odd look passing between the brothers. I watched him walk away, glad to have our space to ourselves again, though his presence hadn't been the intrusion it normally was for me. I leaned against Jase, relaxing as the stress of such an enormous day left me. I let my shoulders droop, settling. Auroras danced behind the ice, beautiful and serene.

*I wished I could be like them, dancing high above it all.*

Light footsteps and a high-pitched giggle broke my peace. I swivelled, frowning at the source of the sound. A pretty girl with hair piled high sashayed into our space. Jase rose, giving her a small wave. He met her halfway into the grove, sending me a grimace over his shoulder. Slightly reassured, I slid down the rock into the spot Nestor had occupied, resting my back against the granite. I stared out at the skyscape, trying to block out the giggles from the girl and Jase's deep, rumbling voice.

I chanced a quick look back and wished I hadn't. Startling blue eyes stared at me across Jase's chest, narrowing when the girl saw me looking. She tilted her head back, one hand brushing Jase's shoulder. Her hips moved, sliding in a mesmerising way I knew I could never replicate. Jase said something I couldn't hear, leaning into her, brushing her arm before breaking contact as he backed away.

The girl laughed again. I knew I'd hear that annoying giggle in my dreams tonight. The breath left me as she walked away, keeping Jase's attention. His eyes followed her into the tree line. Not keen to be caught watching them, I turned back to the rainbows. They no longer looked as serene, slamming against the wall of ice as though to break free from their prison.

My lips tightened as he seated himself beside me on the rock. My chest was tight, and I drew in the urge to run, to be alone. My peace had broken in the wake of the day. With a small huff, I made to get up, but Jase's hands on my shoulders prevented me, pressing me back down.

Rather than sink into my patch of moss, I kept my back rigid—until Jase's hands slid up my neck, squeezing gently. I remembered his hands on my calves, sliding beneath my skirts this afternoon and shivered as strong fingers sank into my hair, massaging my scalp. I let out a small moan, leaning back. His dark chuckle almost had me bolting upright, but his fingers twined in the roots of my hair tugged—playfully, not so playfully—and I tilted my head back, giving him full access.

Skilful fingertips brushed across my brow, running down the sides of my face to my shoulders, gently manipulating the muscles there. He dragged his hands back to the base of my skull, tipping my head back to expose my throat, but he didn't touch me there. Nothing was predatory about him. Instead, his touch was calming.

His thumbs moved in firm circles from the base of my skull to the top of my head, tugging at my hair, releasing tension there. Gently he resumed his earlier task, untangling my hair, though it must have been a mess and began braiding it. His fingers twisted the strands, reminding me of how he had twined the vines in my Ark yesterday. Had it only been yesterday? I yawned, just thinking about it. His chest rumbled again.

"Sleepy, V?"

"Mmhm." I murmured, snuggling deeper. He finished the plait and tied it off, tucking the ends into the art he'd made of my hair. I leaned my head against his flax-clad thigh, breathing him in, wishing I could spend a night in those arms. But with Mal as his father... I closed my eyes, enjoying the moment he'd given me.

The events of the day tumbled over in my mind, no matter how hard I tried to blank them out. With respect, it had been a rather big one. My Bidding, the Vault—nausea rose just at the thought of it. Jase stroked his hand across my shoulders. Perhaps he read the tension rising there.

Something from the day sat poorly with me, and I turned to face Jase.

"You knew." The words came out flat. I turned, pulling my hair from his fingers. I wanted to see him when he answered; to know he, at least, would tell me the truth.

"Knew what?" Jase's brow dipped in confusion.

"That Nestor had been in the Vault before."

Expecting denial, I was surprised when Jase nodded.

"When?' I pressed, trying to read his face.

Jase sat there, tight-lipped. I leaned further back, and he slipped down beside me, curving his back against the rock. I rested a light hand on his arm, half expecting him to push me away, but he didn't. Those same arms I had dreamed about in the Vault. I shook my head for focus, waiting for him to speak.

Jase breathed out a long sigh. Suddenly I knew something terrible was coming.

"Nestor– after our mother died, it was…difficult," Jase began and faltered. I slipped my hand down into his. He squeezed tight, sucking in a deep breath.

"Nestor," he closed his eyes tight, "he spent a lot of time in the Vault…after–," he couldn't continue, and I dipped my head to slide inside those wide shoulders, wrapping my arms about his chest. The steady thump of his heart couldn't stop the poison of what came next.

"Our father sent him there."

My mind boggled. Still leaning into Jase's chest, I let my arms drop until they hit his waist, the edges of his pants. I backed away, flabbergasted.

"What?"

"Our father–,"

"Mal."

"–sent my brother to the Vault–,"

"Why?"

"To die."

Jase sank down the rock, the heels of his hands pressing into his eyes. Tears flowed around them, and I wondered if he had ever spoken about this to anyone at all.

He continued, and this time I didn't interrupt.

"Nestor lost it after our mother died. He was the one who found her, trapped in the ice." Jase looked up at me with pleading eyes. "They said the Earth," he coughed, "that the Earth punished her for her cr...crimes."

His head bowed into my lap. I curved over him, drawing him down to the stone bench he had dragged from the Hall under cover of the night sky for me so I wouldn't be sitting in the dirt, a barrier between Her and me.

His arms curled around my legs, holding tight as though I anchored him from being swept away.

"What crimes?" The words sat poorly on my tongue.

Jase shrugged, pale dreads brushing the ground. I cupped his face in my hands, looking into those liquid eyes I'd known for so long, waiting.

"Nestor never said a word. No matter what our father threatened him with, he never spoke. I've never seen such strength, such bravery," he kept his eyes on mine, "until I saw you stand up to him. To Ma– to Dad."

I rocked back on the bench, hands falling from his face. My eyes searched his.

"So...what happened?"

"Do you remember the summer when Nestor was...conspicuously absent?"

I did. Jase grinned recalling, I was certain, of the first time we had been alone in each other's company. Afternoons spent leaping into the lake from the rock, drying beneath the rainbows, hands clasped, whispering secrets we never thought would be important. It was the summer we had began the tradition of eating separately from the rest of the community.

It had also been the first time I had shown him one of my Creations—a simple pea seedling curling around my finger like a ring on my command, much like the ones the Keepers wore.

His laughter has been all the confirmation I had needed. Creating at will, his approval egging me on. Set on a course that led me here today. Tears traced his cheeks, and I wiped them away.

"My f– Mal sent him there, to the Vault, when Nestor wouldn't admit to killing her." It came out in a rush, as though the words had been bottled away for so long, he wasn't sure they would come out quite right. "He wandered into the catacombs, lost in the darkness for three days. Dad refused to go in. I looked for him, screaming his name until I had no voice left. No one else dared enter. Cowards." He spat. "Then I found him, curled in a pile of bones and shrouds, trying to keep warm though it was stiflingly hot down there."

His head tilted, and my hands followed it, smoothing his hair. The memory of the dead earth was so fresh I couldn't help but see Nestor, so much younger, frightened, and alone. So similar to me. Had he helped me out of pity during my Bidding, seeing himself before his father in the Hall?

"But you got him out?" I wondered how they thought Nestor had frozen his mother as I struggled to keep up with the details of Jase's story. How could I have lived here all my life and not known about their mother? Jase spoke again, disrupting my thoughts.

"I carried him through the tunnels, past the Keepers, into the Hall." His eyes wandered, lost in the memory, seeing something I wasn't privy to. "Most of the families had assembled there. They watched me take him, and not one raised a hand to help. I carried him home, washed him, fed him. He suffered a fever for a week. I feared he would die."

Those liquid eyes stared at me, revealing his uncertainty of the world he had grown up in, for a moment reverting to a seventeen-year-old boy on the cusp of manhood, taking on an older man's mantle. Fury built in me at their father. What man could do that to his sons—so rare, yet he had two he didn't deserve.

"You're too kind, chasing after people like Nestor and me," I said with a smile to soften the words. He smiled back.

"But, you're the people I love."

I bit my lip, searching his eyes. I knew I should be relieved that I had family in this stupidly loyal, kind-hearted man, but I didn't. I wanted something far more. Then another thought occurred to me.

"Why did they—Mal—blame him? Nestor?"

Jase buried his head in my lap so I could barely distinguish his words.

"Because he found her. And I didn't."

# Chapter Eleven

A sharp rap on the glass told me the Keeper was outside, waiting on me. The morning light illuminated the frosted glass, my Creations having receded this morning, seeming to sense my need for time alone. I dressed quickly, still processing Jase's story from last night, my short period of incarceration. My thoughts turned to my present, trepidation warring with excitement.

The Library. Did the Keepers know my desire to view the frozen rows of books, to see if the Library held up to the legends surrounding it? My head still cluttered with thoughts, I wondered if I would ever have it clear again.

Blinking in the bright sunlight, I smiled uncertainly at the Keeper, glad to see the woman from yesterday. She smiled kindly.

"I will take you to the Library. Mal is...perhaps not the best person for you to deal with right now.

You made quite an impression on him, as always."

I vividly remembered the handprint I'd left in the centre of his robes, blushing.

"Why would you stand up for me?"

Dark eyes considered me, and I faltered for a moment, recalling Sandrine's obscure comment of lending me assistance.

"I mean, why now?"

"You have always had some...assistance with your sentencing. It has been our duty to care for you since your parents disappeared."

I frowned at her.

"My parents died."

The Keeper shook her silver striped head. "No, child. Your parents disappeared when you were but a babe. We cared for you until you came of age, old enough to live your own life. But we still have a hand in your...fate, when it is necessary."

I stared at her, my thoughts racing. She'd dropped the biggest surprise of my life and yet stood there, calm, surveying me as I absorbed it. Well, I tried to. A stray hair tickled my face, and I shoved it back, annoyed.

"No, that's not right. You– you Keepers told me

they died! Everyone knows that."

She gazed at me with a small measure of pity. My stomach curled as though it were full of parasites. I gripped the edge of my Ark tightly, determined not to drop, listening hard to her next words, but nothing seemed to stick in my mind.

"That was always the plan. But now you must go into the Library, and it is time you learned the truth."

I gaped at her, barely able to comprehend what she was saying. If my parents had disappeared, then where did they go? Had they been exiled, or had the Earth eaten them in recompense for some slight? Questions bubbled up inside me, but one thought floated in my mind.

*Did Jase and Nestor know?*

"Are they still alive?"

The words tumbled from my mouth before I could catch them. My jaws snapped shut on my tongue, but I was too numb to feel it.

Their family had been Keepers for generations, after all. Surely the boys would have figured out if something was off when my parents had disappeared. But they had been young, after all. Jase was only slightly older than me, while Nestor and I were of an age together.

I followed the Keeper past the Hall to the plateau behind it. The Green was busy this morning, the baker bustling about, preparing food for midday fare, musicians playing loudly. I thought of Nestor, but it was brief and passed in the wake of what loomed over me, my time in the Library. A sentence, a threat? Or a chance to draw truth hidden from us by the very people we were supposed to trust the most.

At the far end, past the artisans, a lone building stood tall, blocking the view of snow-tipped mountains behind it. Great glass windows decorated its sides—scenes of people and animals from a history long since lost, its secrets locked away inside.

I would learn those secrets.

The Green was silent as we crossed, eyes following every step we took. Heat rose in my cheeks again. On the far side of the Green, Jase and Nestor were in animated conversation with one of the growers, so engrossed neither had noticed the strangled silence thickening the air.

The grower did and paused. The boys turned to see the cause of his distraction. Nestor's eyes followed me, and I ignored the urge to scratch at my skin. I caught Jase's eye. He grinned at me, ignoring the looks we drew.

In the shadow of the massive fig that housed the Hall, I shivered. No rainbow light penetrated here. We passed beyond it, mounting whitewashed steps to a broad, arched entry. The Keeper lifted a bronze ring stuck to the middle of the door and let it drop.

The sound echoed as quick footsteps approached us from the other side. I shifted from side to side, nervous and uncomfortable, not knowing what to expect. Thoughts of my parents swirled in my mind, and I broke from the desire to race away from the Library, down the stone steps, and find out what I could about them, but the Keeper had said the answers I needed were here. As though reading my mind, the Keeper placed a hand on my arm in admonishment. I stilled, breathing in through my nose as the footsteps reached the door. Several clicks sounded on the other side, and I wondered how many locks a place with great glass windows would need.

With the ominous groan of disuse, the door opened, scraping the floor. It had drooped on its hinges, and no one fixed it. My forehead creased, and I made a mental note to ask Jase about it. Everything in our community was in perfect working order. Everything well maintained as a gratitude for our freedom. But this revered building wasn't being looked after at all. I peered into the dim light that filtered out, surprised when a wispy head appeared in my vision, no higher than my hips.

Before me stood quite possibly the smallest woman I had ever seen in my life.

# Chapter Twelve

The halo of wispy hair bobbed, a thin arm lifting a candle to peer at us through thick lenses perched across a narrow face. As she turned to face the Keeper, her hair swung out past sharp shoulders, seeming to brush across the tip of the flame. I wondered for a moment if she had ever set it on fire, inspecting the edges for a gap or frizzled edges, but it was such a wild mass I could barely see the woman beneath it. A fine glass bell covered the candle. She held it in a steady hand, raising it to inspect us as she drew us into the gloom.

"Galyna." Her voice was soft and croaky, as though it wasn't used very often. I looked at the Keeper in surprise, feeling rude. I'd never asked her name. Somehow it suited her, standing strong and calm as I imagined she would against any chaos.

"Leurona," Galyna inclined her head, brushing her fingers against my arm. "Remember to seek the truth, Veritas. In all its forms. You will know what to do."

I looked at her, eyes wide. I blinked, ready with questions I should have asked before but had misused the time, lost in my thoughts and excitement, but she was already moving across the Green. Surprisingly speedy when she wanted to be. I snorted. Footsteps echoed away into the darkness, and I hurried after Leurona, not keen to be stuck in an unknown dark place without light. I jumped as the door closed behind me.

Quick steps caught me up to the wispy woman who strode along at a brisk pace. Did everyone have to walk so fast? It seemed I was determined to be grumpy. I cast about for a distraction and came up empty.

"You're the Librarian?"

*Original, V. Great intro.*

"Yes."

I peered at her, waiting for more information, but it seemed one word was the limit of her skills.

Oh, this was going to be a great conversation.

The little light only illuminated a pace before us. I could only imagine Leurona knew where she was going from her years of service. The dark was impenetrable. The thought sat oddly with me for a moment before I figured out why.

"The windows!" I spluttered inelegantly. "You've covered them all up!"

We stopped as the Librarian placed the light in an alcove, brightening a stone section of the wall. I looked around for books, but in the tiny room, there was nothing else to be seen. I turned back to Leurona and came nose-to-nose with her, grey hairs reaching for my face. With a cry, I shot backwards, tripping over my own feet and landing hard on my backside. It was becoming rather bruised.

I scrambled back to my feet, dusting myself off. The Librarian shuffled a square stone against the wall. I frowned, wondering if she used it to speak to people—when no one was here to converse with— or if she needed it to reach things. I imagined stones stacked around the edges of the Library and determined not to trip on anything else.

"The light is kept out."

Her croaky voice bounced off the walls. I was reminded again of the Vault, wondering how big the room really was. I coughed, trying to gather myself, but the tiny Librarian had unsettled me.

"I can see that." My pun fell flat. "Ah– *why* is the light kept out?"

"In case it melts the books." She slipped sideways into the dark and disappeared, leaving me alone in the alcove. I looked around, waiting for her to come back, but there was no sound, not even a footstep.

Surely this was some kind of joke. Perhaps she amused herself at the expense of those sent to her? Unless I was in for another surprise, I hadn't ever heard of anyone in my lifetime sent to the Library as punishment. How long had this little woman been here, alone in the dark? Her appearance and voice certainly suggested she wasn't used to company.

I turned around in the alcove, not daring to step into the dark. A small bench leant against one wall on rusty legs. Tentatively I took a seat and waited.

By the time Leurona came to collect me, I had curled up on the bench to sleep and awoke with a thumping headache. My mouth was parched, and I eagerly gulped the water she handed me. I drained the cup and made to hand it back. She shook her head.

"Yours now."

A woman of few words.

"Thank you?"

She shrugged, disappearing into the darkness. I called out, determined not to be abandoned in the little room again. A flicker of light caught my attention, and without really thinking it through, I dashed in that direction, nearly running over her. I gasped, trying to catch my balance and leaned onto an object in an effort not to bowl her over.

"Off. Off!" She flapped her hands at me, and I straightened up. Magnified eyes stared at me for a long moment. Finally, she reached up, pulling a string dangling near the sliver of light I had followed. With a hefty tug, she drew it down.

Louvers along one wall shone open, folding back on themselves. Leurona pulled a second string. A mighty clang echoed around the room as the louvers retreated to the ceiling. Coloured light filtered in, creating patterns that crisscrossed the floors, populated with rows tables and chairs. There wasn't a book in sight. I opened my mouth to query the lack of what made a library a library when the windows caught my eyes. The images glowed, illuminated as though brought to life. Stories of the Library's windows weren't exaggerated at all.

The images were bright and clear, with a blue tinge. Outside it must be evening. I had slept for quite a while then. Leurona crossed the hall, going through the same process on the other side. With both sides of the hall exposed, coloured light danced in the space between the two windows, creating a dizzying kaleidoscope.

Tables and chairs filled the space, straight and unused. Every desk was bare, save one. Pots and writing equipment covered the one nearest us. I looked at Leurona. She nodded at me and smiled.

"Now, we work."

By the time I had copied out the pages she had set before me—all from loose sheets, not a single bound volume in sight—my fingers were stiff and cramped. I honestly wasn't sure what her work was. So far, I had made lists of numbers with columns of names next to them. Leurona moved me around the table beneath different sections of the window and had me fill the paper in accordance with how the light fell.

The result was a patched mess. I wasn't sure how anyone would ever be able to understand it. Nor was I sure this the window's function in the past. Not that anyone would know, with all that information kept secret and locked away.

I peered to the back of the Library, where Leurona had disappeared behind a door. I hadn't seen her since she set me my task. I looked around again to check she hadn't crept up on me stood, stretching my arms and neck. Everything seemed stiff, and several things that shouldn't have popped.

Still stretching, I walked over the nearest stained window. The colours amazed me. Various animals alternated with men in strange poses. I'd have to find the cat one to describe to Jase later on. A pang struck me, and I paused, seeking distraction in the window before me. A man walked next to a four-legged beast. Words decorated the edges, none like I had ever seen. I wished I knew what they said. Would it be the story of the man and his animal? His name, where he was going?

Movement beyond the window broke my reverie. I pressed against the base of the window where a single, flat section lay uncoloured. A white blur slid by—Jase. I had raised my hand to attract his attention when I realised I was wrong. The blur stopped just paces from me, on the other side of the window.

The wall separated us, and I was glad of it as a girl I'd never seen before turned to face me. Eyes as black as the darkness that had pervaded the Vault stared through me, set into a face that was as old but appeared young. Long, straw-like hair faded white as though with time laid limp over fragile looking skin. I shivered, covering my chest as though expecting her to reach through the wall to touch me. Those eyes knew of years I didn't. She seemed ageless, skin pale and light, seemingly brittle as a winter leaf.

She stared at me for a moment longer then walked on, becoming a blur again. I shook my head, looking around. The light behind the window was growing bright. I blinked, wondering how long I had been standing there, staring. Perhaps it had been a dream? I returned to the desk as Leurona appeared in the doorway.

Leurona said nothing as she passed by me,

unwrapping the string from a complicated knot, tugging the louvers down. Darkness pervaded the space again, and my chest tightened. I called out questions as she retreated, but no answers came. I counted her footsteps as she returned to the door, locking me out, and wondered what on earth I was supposed to do.

By the third day, I had worked out how to use the lamp and discovered a rug hiding beneath one of the desks. It made sleep a little easier as writing, and the darkness strained both my temper and my eyes. I had also discovered a basin and a small privy near the door as I scuffled around it, trying to pry it open. When Leurona went through her routine on the fourth day, I had more questions and stood in her path to prevent her from deserting me.

"Let me in to the Library." My tone was polite but firm.

"You are in the Library."

"No, I'm not. This isn't the Library, is it? It's behind that door—it's underneath." This last was a guess, but I knew the building wasn't that big from the outside.

Leurona inclined her head, hair swaying.

Nodding, she took the lamp from me, leading the way to the door. I held my breath as she unlocked it with a key she stowed in her robes. The door opened a crack, and she slipped through it, closing it quickly and locking it before I could wrench it open again.

I swore and cursed, slamming my fists against the wood until they were as sore as the rest of me. I slid down the door, tired and defeated. What was the point of sending me here, if I wasn't going to learn anything? I sat in the dark, pressing the heels of my hands into my eyes. I was sick, so thoroughly *sick* of being left alone in the dark.

Warmth pressed against my eyelids, brightness growing. For a moment, I thought Leurona had returned through a secret door—I wouldn't put it past her, the way she crept about—and raised my head to rant at her. A good rant was exactly what I needed. I missed Jase's company more than ever.

But it wasn't the frazzled little Librarian that confronted me. Instead, a glowing orb bobbed about, level with my nose. My mini-sun was back. My hands warmed again, and soon, I had a dozen suns hovering about me. I smiled at their company, and they jingled back.

Now I had a chance of finding a way into the Library proper.

Three broken fingernails, a stubborn rusty lock, and a broken cup later, I was no closer to my goal than when I started. I stared at the door, convinced I would never see the books. I fumed inwardly at Leurona and her books—*melt them, my backside*—there was nothing for the heat of the day to melt! Everything I craved was hidden away behind that door. I glared at it.

A growl started in my throat. Sucking in deep breaths through my nose, I racked my brain. A tiny bell rang near my ear. One of my suns floated by, bobbing. It pressed against my cheek then pulled away, hovering at the door.

I rose to my feet, uncertain. The little ball dropped to the lock, pressing against it. Very slowly, it slid inside, disappearing. A bright light shone from the small space. The rest of the suns bobbed together, jingling merrily.

One by one, the suns slid through the lock until I was left in darkness again. I shivered, not sure if it was from a chill in the air or the absence I felt without them. The door creaked, and I jumped, certain Leurona would berate me for destroying her door or for Creating. The door opened, and a little sun bobbed around it. I smiled, slipping my hand around it, enjoying its warmth.

The rest clustered together, joining into one light and, as I had done in the Vault, shrank down. The one I held joined its kin. It illuminated a staircase leading down, chiselled stone with no railing. I descended carefully.

As I turned through the long staircase, my sun's light reflected on something below. Reaching the bottom, I exhaled, my breath puffing in tiny clouds in front of me. Gooseflesh raised on my forearms, and the sun bobbed at chest height, radiating warmth. Surely the books would be here?

I brought my sun higher, letting it float several paces in front of me. Row upon row of broad iced blocks stretched into the darkness. Ignoring the cold, I approached one. Inside their prison lay the books. Our history, our knowledge all locked away.

My fingers tingled, and I looked down, surprised to see them pressed against the ice. They came away slippery. I leaned in closer, trying to read the words on the spines of the books, but the ice was too thick. The images wavered, unreadable.

A noise startled me, and I jumped heart hammering. I stared into the ice, reflecting a person standing behind me. I gritted my teeth.

"Leurona."

"Veritas."

I startled; I hadn't realised the Librarian knew my name. I spun to face her, my frustrations and anger building. Unfortunately, she beat me to it.

"You brought light. YOU BROUGHT LIGHT INTO MY LIBRARY!" She shrieked. I covered my ears, backing into the frozen stacks. Eyes bulging, hair standing out on end, she appeared quite demented.

"I– I'm sorry," I stammered, collecting the little sun in my palm, attempting to hide it and failing magnificently. She opened her mouth—for another tirade perhaps, but I was tired and frustrated too.

"You left me up there alone, in the dark, for four days! I'm the one who should be yelling at you!"

Leurona raised a pointed finger at me, but I didn't give her the chance to get started.

"You left me with some stupid job I'm sure isn't what it's supposed to be, stuffing notes on a page and turning in circles all night long," I glared at her, and she backed up a step, "leaving me a blanket to sleep in I'm lucky I found. So don't you dare tell me I shouldn't do this or that!"

Rage left me as quickly as it had come. I'd be sent back to the Vault for certain; now I'd abused the Librarian. I wanted to whisper an apology, but I'd expended all the energy I had. Instead, I cupped my hands around the little sun, wishing it were cold, but light. Nothing changed. I closed my eyes again, thinking of the frozen rainbows in the sky above us, the rows of books encased in ice.

When I opened my eyes, the little sun glowed a dim blue. I waved my hand over it, feeling no heat. A cold sun. I held it out to Leurona, who inspected it, running her hands around it but never touching it. I bit back a grin. Perhaps she wasn't the only crazy in this place.

Finally satisfied, Leurona led me down the rows of books. There were so many; I lost count. Suddenly I was glad of my sun should I be lost down here if Leurona stole away with the light again.

We reached the end of one of the long rows, stopping beneath a domed ceiling covered in glass.

I recognised it as one of the skylights the Sky People used—an improvement from the previous Librarian, perhaps? There was so much I didn't know.

Leurona pulled a lever attached to the wall, and the skylight opened, letting in the daylight. Rainbows reflected through the mosaic of thick glass above, scattering onto the frozen shelves. Row after row glistened, truths and stories hidden inside.

*Melt the books, my butt.* She'd put the light directly on the rows of ice. So much for all the pomp and fanfare above in the outer hall. Leurona turned the lever, rotating it. The glass above us spun, sending a kaleidoscope of colours dancing across the room. The rows stretched back further than I could see.

*Why?*

My unspoken question echoed, drowning out everything else. After a moment, the Librarian stopped the glass turning. Frozen crystal glinted in the wan light. She watched the light flicker across her wards, her glasses reflecting white. Paired with her hair, it gave her a madder look than usual.

"Why are the books kept away from us? What can't we know about our past?"

My demands tumbled out, unbidden. My chest clenched as I waited on the answers I hadn't known I needed.

Leurona started at me, her eyes alight with some inner fervour.

"Long ago, there was a great storm—the Last Storm. The world came alive. So many died...few lived. A select few..." she drifted off. I was so desperate for answers I dared not interrupt her.

"The one who froze the sky imprisoned us. Now we live at the mercy of Her bidding."

"Who?" I whispered.

"The Earth," the Librarian continued dreamily. "She sees us, what we did, what we are doing," those glowing eyes turned on me, "and so we hid away, like frightened children before a vengeful god. But some," her voice grew suddenly strong, "decided others could live. Others like you."

"Me?"

What did I have to do with this?

"You and your Creations can save this world. Melt the sky. Free us."

I stared at her. She was crazier than I thought. And I was stuck down here with her for who knew how long.

"The books." I persisted, "Why did they have to freeze the books?"

"To stop anyone from knowing, of course."

"From knowing *what*?"

"To know who froze the sky, who will bring back the rain."

Leurona smiled at me benevolently. I shook my head at her, not comprehending. Was I supposed to make it rain? Why was it so forbidden?

"Read them."

She gestured to the books. I gaped at her. Did she want me to melt the ice? Surely that would flood this area, destroy the pages in their cages.

Leurona drifted away, toward one of the long racks of books. Here the tomes looked older, their wavering forms rippling through the ice. Chains surrounded each book. These were already locked away. Why do it twice?

She walked around the corner of the nearest row and disappeared. I followed her around the corner, expecting to see her on the other side. But try as I might, my crazy companion was conspicuously absent. I stamped my foot in frustration. When would she stop with these ridiculous games? I found my thirst for knowledge greatly diminished.

I wanted to be back in my greenhouse beneath real light, hands in the earth, where I felt most at home. I wanted to see Jase's grin again, to rant about Nestor, share bread beneath the twilight sky. My eyes closed, I leaned on the ice behind me, and slid sideways.

And right into the crazy-haired Librarian, who grinned at me like I had passed a test. I rose to my feet, taking in my surroundings. We stood inside the wall of ice. It was nothing more than a facade. The row of books stood before me free of any enclosure, save their chains. Leurona dangled a key from gnarled fingers.

"The ice keeps the dust off the books."

I stared at her, then at the books. My fingers rose, but I paused, not quite touching the ancient covers. Leurona slipped the key into the lock, moving away.

"You have seen Her."

I nodded, speechless, remembering the odd figure I'd seen through the stained-glass windows.

Leurona smiled a fanatical thing that shook me.

"She is always seen before an event, one that has changed the world. These are stories of Her. Here," she brought down a faded, blue-covered book, "this tells of Her return."

I gently laid a finger on it, lest it crumbled under my touch. The cover was soft, padded. Leurona flicked open the book to a page well marked. Fingerprints and splotches marred the edges where they curled and cracked. I wondered how many Librarians had looked over this beautifully written page.

*When two hearts bend*
*The Kingdom will call,*
*Eternity falls.*
*Feather to ash,*
*Blackest of heart.*
*The beast takes a hold*
*To overcome the soul.*
*Death is conquered*
*'Til immortality reigns.*
*Shadows rise*
*Waters fall*
*Time shifts*

*Until the waters rise again.*

*As it began, so must it end.*

It all sounded pretty, but I couldn't see mention of the white-haired girl anywhere. Leurona nodded at the page, pressing a sharp nail against the end of the third stanza.

"Here," she murmured, "This part is you. Create the world," her voice had taken on that dreamy quality again, "A perfect world. Destroy this one." She added.

I gaped at her in horror.

Leurona left. I shut my mouth with a snap, studying the book, the key nestled into the spine. I slipped it over my head, re-reading the poem until my eyes blurred. More books, similar to the one I held, leaned into the gap Leurona had created when she removed this one. I freed them from their chains, pulling each one down, flicking through as many as I could, but they were all the same, filled with the verse that made no sense to me at all.

Volumes piled beside me, and I shifted onto my back, resting my head on them, balancing the larger tomes on my knees. When the daylight began to dim, I slept where I lay, beginning my task again when I awoke. I wasn't thirsty down here, or hungry.

Perhaps the ice had something to do with it, ice that shouldn't exist. So many questions filled me with a longing to read everything, a craving I couldn't satisfy. I wasn't sure what I was looking for—and hoped I would know when I found it.

I had made it almost to the end of the row when a section of dates out of place stopped me. Inspecting the row, I cursed, furious with myself for not seeing the pattern earlier. Luerona had catalogued the books according to linage.

Galyna had said my answers were here. I had thought she meant my parents. But what if she had meant family in the sense of genealogy?

Leurona had said it was about me, had intimated my line froze the sky. I struggled with the concept that one person could harness so much power—but that was all so long ago—I'd need to be looking at books over three hundred years old. I slipped inside the ice case. Amazed at how much colder it was on the outside than in with the books. Almost as though they breathed with a life of their own.

I hauled down a stack of books, opening family

trees. I traced the ages through—the generation after the Last Storm marked clearly in bright blue ink. I trailed my finger down the page, looking at years. The system changed after that; I supposed that with so much death and chaos, record-keeping wasn't at its best. The dates stopped at the bottom of the page, and I flicked to the next one, but it was blank.

Annoyed, I kept flicking, but the rest of the pages were empty. I tossed the book unceremoniously aside and opened the next. The Last Storm was again clearly marked, generations listed to the bottom of the page. But the next one was empty, and the next. I opened volume after volume, turning quickly to that line of blue ink, knowing with certainty, the next page would be blank.

A tower of books quickly grew beside me until I tossed the last one in anger. It slammed into the uneven structure, toppling it in a flurry of pages. I sighed, angry with myself for damaging the books. Rising to my feet, I stretched cramped muscles, leaning too far back. My shoulder caught the edge of the shelf above, and books came tumbling down.

I reached down again, out of breath and cross—

and paused. The book that lay on my feet had an unusual symbol on the cover, like an eye. I turned it around, running my fingers over it. It reminded me of something, but I couldn't put my finger on it. Flicking it open, I immediately knew this book was significant. Like with the prophecy—poem—fingerprints dotted the opening pages. Many Librarians had studied this line. I shivered, flicking through it. The family tree was so much larger than the others. Every now and then, the eye symbol appeared beside a name. I traced from the Last Storm to the bottom of the page, prepared for yet another blank spread.

Ink covered the page, generations running down it, very short, with few offspring. I flicked the next page and stopped. Two names I recognised intertwined on the page with a single line denoting a child. I touched my name reverently, tracing back to my parents. Nika Silman and Emil Tempestas. I blinked back tears, wondering where they were—if they were still alive.

The eye was pencilled lightly beside my name as though unsure whether I warranted it or not. A tiny dot appeared in the centre, and the image hit me like a slap in the face. Jase had drawn this symbol in the "A" of my greenhouse, my Ark. As a joke, he had said.

He had known this symbol—known it represented my family and me. Something quailed inside me as I wondered what else he hadn't shared with me. I wasn't sure if I was curious or angry. Inhaling through my nose, I rested against the shelf and picked up the next book out of habit.

Flicking the pages idly, I paused at the blue line again and turned the page. This one was filled, too, going on several pages. I flicked forward, interested to see who was at the end of the line. I paused at the end of the page, staring at the final union and its progeny.

Nestor and Jase's names lined the bottom of the page. Next to Jase's, a faint line marked a union. Puzzled, I peered closer, trying to make it out. My blue sun drifted down, giving me the extra light to read it. I never did get to see the name that so tentatively joined to Jase's; the tiny eye symbol was enough.

Standing abruptly, I scattered the books in all directions, no longer caring where they fell. I grabbed the two with Jase and my genealogies and raced up the stairs, hollering for Leurona as I went. Slamming open the door at the top like it was paper-thin, I strode into the darkened hall.

"Leurona!" I yelled, sure she was here somewhere. I couldn't see a damned thing and grabbed the string, yanking the louvers off the windows. Daylight filtered in, and I breathed. I realised I hadn't known if it was night or day, or even how many days I had been with the books. My stomach rumbled as I searched for Leurona.

She sat at one of the tables, surrounded by Keepers. I halted, unsure of what to do. That they would sit in the dark with her struck me. So many things were wrong in this place. I had come here expecting to find answers but instead was left with more questions than I could ever have imagined.

The small group stared at me as though I was something unusual to be studied. I remembered the eye next to my name, my name next to Jase's, and strode to the table, slamming the books down.

"Why is my name linked with your family, Mal?" I growled, anger flowing through me, hot enough to melt all the ice in the Library.

Mal canted his head, still studying me. In a detached voice, he ruined the only friendship I held dear.

"We wanted to see what would happen."

The rage turned cold in my veins, immobilising me. My blue sun multiplied before me, as though all the tiny ones inside were tired of being clustered together. Mal eyed them but made no attempt to rise.

"You wanted to– to see–," I spluttered the words, took a breath, and started again, but it still didn't come out right. "We are not an…an EXPERIMENT!"

Four sets of eyes watched me, judged me. Rage rose in me, not the red fury of the moment before but a calmness that descended on me like a blanket, numbing the world. I was so tired of not knowing, not understanding who I was. That somehow, I was *wrong.* A chill raced through me, leaving my skin icy. I left the books on the table, striding to the door.

"Where are you going?" Mal raised his voice for the first time, but I was tired of his rules and this place that made no sense to me at all.

I faced him with a smile I knew was as cold as my heart. He recoiled though I stood halfway across the long room. Not a soul moved. A faint humming echoed around the closed space, and I realised it came from Leurona. Her words bounced around my mind.

Build a better world.

*A perfect one.*

Cold and detached, I faced the father of the man who I loved the most. *Had* loved, because none of it was real. My suns bobbed around me, blazing blue. The air frosted, and I wondered if they had brought the icy air with them. Then I shuddered, fingers turning to frost, and realised it was coming from me. The ice reminded me of the story of Nestor's mother, and how she had died, what Mal had done to his youngest son afterwards. Suddenly, I wasn't cold, though the air inside the Library was unnaturally still.

"You want to keep the knowledge hidden, to keep us from knowing what you planned? Tell me why there are only a few family lines left. Tell me what happened to them."

The four stood mute as I waited, still expecting answers.

"Then, let me know how you feel about being

locked *in*."

This last came out as a whisper. Ice flowed from my fingertips, coating the flagstones in front of me. It spread toward the Keepers as I retreated, kicking the door open. Ice covered the walls, thickening until it resembled the book stacks below. The Keepers followed Leurona in a mad dash to the door that led to the underground stacks. I wondered if being down there would save them, and decided I didn't care. Ice slicked the roof, coating the coloured glass, freezing everything inside.

# Chapter Thirteen

I crossed the Green, walking straight through the middle. Heads turned, but no one approached me. Ice cracked as it covered the top of the tall building I'd just left, with the Keepers still inside. The only movement came from across the sparsely populated area. As I reached the edge of the plateau, I turned to look back at my work. Nestor caught my eye, gesturing at me with an open mouth. I smirked, pleased to have shocked him for once.

The Library resembled nothing more than one of the frosted book stacks buried deep within its innards. Rainbows reflected across its surface, cast blue beneath the frozen sky. I smiled, remembering Leurona's words.

*A perfect world.*

My smile grew bigger as I headed down the hill. Maybe her crazy was contagious.

As I reached the bottom of the hill, a shadow

flickered in the greenhouse windows. I paused, peering in, wondering if I would see the strange girl again. The dead gaze of her eyes haunted but fascinated me. A blonde head appeared in the window, but it wasn't the girl. Jase waved and gestured me inside.

I stared at him for a moment, unsmiling. It occurred to me he had no idea what I had just done. As I passed beneath the doorway, the sign he'd hung over it so many moons ago drew my attention. Its sharp angles marred by curved edges, the eye stood out so much more now. I jumped, yanking at the sign until it sat in my hands. Jase opened the door with a quick grin.

"They let you out!"

He enveloped me in a bear hug, and for a second, I stood there, breathing in his warmth. Then I remembered everything I had learned and poked him in the chest with the sign.

He took it from me, sighing.

"It came down? I'll put it back up later on. I've been watering your plants, making sure they didn't die..." He trailed off as I placed a finger over the A, tracing the curves of the symbol he'd put there.

His shaggy head hung down, shoulders expanding as he took long breaths. Slowly he raised his eyes, meeting my gaze. Usually azure eyes were dark, unreadable.

"I guess you'd better come inside."

His attitude irked me—inviting me into my own greenhouse. Though I did acknowledge Jase had built the thing in the first place, and I needed to hear what he had to say.

Jase walked to the centre of the greenhouse. Tendrils reached out to tickle him, but he batted them away. He ran a hand through his dreads, pushing them away.

"They didn't let you out, did they."

"No."

"V– this, it goes back a long way, further than you or I."

"But it's going to end with us," I countered, remembering the faint line joining our names in his family genealogy.

Jase shrugged.

"Maybe. I don't know. We *can't* know the future, V. No matter how much *they* want to," I knew he meant his father and the other Keepers, playing with our fates. "They might want to force us together, but honestly, I have never forced anything with you."

He stepped towards me, placing the plaque on top of some plants who threw it off. It clattered to the floor, snapping in two. Jase appeared not to notice as he closed the distance between us. Reaching out to snag my waist, he drew me into him. I bit my lip, pressing my hands on his chest. This was not how I had wanted this conversation to go. Not that I minded terribly, my misgivings of the moment before quelled by his presence.

Jase's other hand caught my chin, brushing his fingers along my jaw. His breath was warm on my lips. My eyes drifted shut, my head tilting back. His lips brushed against mine, gentle, sweet, then more insistent. I gasped, and his tongue slid past my lips, stroking, swirling against mine in a delicate dance. I leaned into him, tangling my hands in his hair. He held me tighter, deepening the kiss. His fingers stroked the nape of my neck, massaging in tiny circles. Blissfully, I lost myself in his arms.

After a time, he broke the contact. A mewling sound escaped my lips, and he chuckled, pressing his forehead against mine. I stared into those blue eyes, bright again, not wanting to lose the moment. Then everything that had happened—the Vault, Nestor, the Library—came crashing into me, slamming me back into reality.

I pulled away.

"What's the eye mean? The symbol?" I added when Jase looked at me with unfocused eyes. He shook his head as though to clear it, reaching for me. I backed away, waiting.

"V– it's nothing, just- I just put it there, looking out. Like I was watching over you." He looked at me to see if I'd bought it.

It was a lame joke and an even lamer lie. I shook my head.

"No."

"No?"

I folded my arms, fighting the urge to stamp my feet, to scream and rage at him. I breathed through my nose sharply, pushing down the madness inside me, but it kept building.

Jase noticed and changed tack.

"You saw the books, right?"

I nodded. He mirrored me.

"It denoted your line, the eye—something about a Seer, back in the day, long, long before the Last Storm. It's followed your family tree the whole way. Apparently, one of my ancestors had some magic ability, too, and they thought pairing us up would be, well...interesting."

I stared at him, a queasiness growing heavy in my gut. He sent a crooked grin my way.

"Aren't you glad it wasn't Nestor?"

The lopsided grin froze on his face as he waited for a response that was never coming. I licked my lips, willing myself not to say it. Desperate to keep it to myself, but it was all too much—just...too many lies.

"You've seen the books."

It was a statement, and it fell flat in the closed space. I suddenly, desperately, needed fresh air. I tried to push past him, but he grabbed my arm, holding me against him. His fingers brushed my cheek, and I closed my eyes, enjoying his touch for a moment—but only a moment. I opened my eyes, pulling away, but his hand remained wrapped around my arm. I wrenched free. His jaw snapped shut with an audible click of teeth.

"V–," he started, reaching for me again. I recoiled. Horror lit his eyes, my stomach flipping as I desperately wished I didn't know. "I know you must feel like it's…like I've…" he floundered, unable to get the words out. I had no such problem.

"Like you've betrayed me?"

The callous words hung around us. That tense feeling of being contained consumed me. I broke out in a sweat, water running over my arms. Only it wasn't water from me. Around us droplets formed, growing into heavy orbs and popping with force, splattering everything near them. A drop hit my lips, and I tasted salt.

It wasn't dew, like in the forest, I realised. It was tears. My tears. Jase stared through it all, straight at me. I wondered if he thought me some sort of freak, someone—something—he had been charged to watch over.

By his father, who hated me.

"Was I just a job? Were you ever my *friend*?" I gestured at him, "and this, you and me- is any of it real?"

Pain speared through me. Throughout it all, my parent's death—I snorted at that myth—living on the edge of society, never being accepted except by one person who had been my rock from the beginning. Always there to comfort me, to offer a quick smile or distraction.

All of it fake.

"You knew," I whispered, "and you never told me."

It wasn't a question.

The pieces fell into place—the mutters of the Keepers, what I'd learned in the Vault, and the Library. Our forbidden history.

*My history.*

My bloodlines. Magic passing through generations, to the end of the world and back. To me.

Water streamed over my cheeks. A dense fog pressed against the roof of the greenhouse, desperate to escape. Pregnant with moisture, it released its burden, right on top of us.

I stared at his wavering figure through the steady downpour of water, distant through the crazed glass created during the Last Storm.

Rain.

I had Created *rain,* which the world hadn't seen

in hundreds of years. Possibility swarmed over me. I stared at my hands. Dirt, which never seemed to lift, floated in little eddies, running over the sides. Rain was fun. I giggled, wiggling my fingers. Ohh, snow! Could I Create that? Humming softly, I swayed to music only I could hear.

Large, warm hands closed over my cold ones. I looked up into Jase's face, stormy eyes staring intensely into mine. I leaned into him, so familiar, then remembered what he'd done.

What he *knew.*

I smiled up at him, noting the concern in the lines around his eyes. My smile became a sneer, and those lines changed.

"V–," he started but never got to finish.

A crack filled the greenhouse. My hand left a nice imprint on his cheek. Water trickled over the mark, already raised and red. I bet it stung. My hand did. It was the first time I had ever hit someone.

Jase stood frozen. Gaze still latched onto mine; he took a very slow step forward. Just as slowly, I backed away, out of his reach. The ground squelched beneath my feet, dirt floating on the surface mixing into mud the more I pressed my feet into the Earth.

I wondered what the comeuppance would be for my actions.

I no longer doubted the rumours of odd deaths and disappearances. After all, what could *get* you out here? In the perfect world, we had no worry of exposure in a temperate climate. But the Keepers were wrong about one thing—they shouldn't have kept my ability to Create from me. Neither should Jase.

"You should have told me." It came out as a hiss, low and vicious.

"I was warned not to tell you," he pleaded, raising his hands at the look that elicited. He shook his head, sun-bleached strands still running with rainwater. I snickered. It was probably the cleanest either of us had been since we were babes.

"It doesn't matter, Jase," I said softly, my giggles subsiding with the rain. "You knew, but you didn't tell me. I should have known in the forest," I realised, "when you laughed. I thought it was just crazy you. But even you aren't mad enough to enrage Her."

The Earth. I couldn't quite say it. But I didn't need

to.

"Your magic comes from the Earth. It's what started all this in the first place!"

Arms spread wide, Jase kicked at a puddle, splashing me with muddy water. Maybe he was crazy, after all. Half a grin sneaked up my face and froze there. I didn't want to fight, but knowing what I did, how could I trust him?

The betrayal squeezed tighter, remembering all the times he'd hugged me after my Biddings, joking with me until the shaking stopped. How he'd cheered me on for Creating something in my greenhouse—the place he had built for *me*.

I'd always assumed Jase had built it as a project for me, as mates—or maybe something more. Those thoughts shattered, along with my trust and most of my heart. What if Jase had built my Ark under orders from the Keepers, from his father. A place to contain me, separate from the rest of the community. Not Outcast, just far enough to be observed. I squeezed my eyes shut. Rivers ran down my cheeks, but the rain had long since ceased.

"V," Jase whispered again, and I opened my eyes.

The world around me was frozen—raindrops

raised from the puddles in streams of ice, just like our frozen sky. For the first time, Jase looked at me in fear. And it hurt.

Typical of me, I turned the fear into something I could use. The hurt, the betrayal, the kiss—it all wound up in my chest, threatening to explode. I swallowed the rest of my tears, chilled on my skin, and stalked towards Jase. To his credit, he didn't retreat.

I pointed a finger at him, listing off everything he'd done, my voice rising to a shriek.

"You knew! You built this place, knowing who I am, what I am! You could have told me something, *anything*, but instead, you take me to the Sky People with their own type of crazy going on, and you let them send me to the Vault? And my parents—I would have loved to have known about them too! What kind of friend are you?" I stopped, lowering my hands and looking him full in the face. My voice cracked. "Or are you my friend at all?"

Jase just shrugged at me, mute. I gaped, expecting more. Then I stopped myself. Why should I expect more from him, given the depth of his betrayal? I shook my head, edging to the door. Some part of me hoped he would stop me, explain that I had it all wrong, but he just stood there, tall and as unmoving as stone.

"Wait- V. What about your parents?"

I sorted, looked at him derisively.

"Please don't say you didn't know they are alive. Just another thi-"

"What?"

"You've kept from me-"

"V- I had no idea. Stop. Just stop!"

Water slushed around my ankles. I looked into the puddle of water on the greenhouse floor and saw myself. Hair curled in the humidity, cheeks flushed. Eyes wide—with panic or excitement? Water beaded at the tips of my fingers and dripped into the puddle, obscuring my face.

From the corner of my eye, I saw movement. Ah, yes. Jase. Yelling and waving his arms as though he mattered. Peace welled inside me. New purpose.

I wanted to cry, to scream, but something else brewed inside me. The walls seemed suddenly close, and I couldn't breathe. I needed fresh air. Shoving at the door, I pushed my way outside. The old lock banged against the glass as the door swung wide, cracking it. With an ominous creak, the jiggered lock finally fell off, hitting the hard soil beneath with a thud. Scratched and damaged, it buried itself halfway into the soil.

I stepped outside the greenhouse. The grass was sharp underfoot, as though it had never known what it could be. Succulent, lush.

*Life.*

I stared at the lock for a moment more, rooted to the ground. So many thoughts roiled in my mind, swirling, confusing. The sky called to me. I tipped my head back, staring at the broad expanse. It looked so large from here, the ice caging us in. How much bigger would it look with nothing between us and the stars, the sun? I wanted to see the moon.

The world was suddenly so much bigger. Why were we stuck in one place? All packed together like bees in a hive. I'd never wanted to explore before, content with my work.

But my purpose *had* changed now, the world of Creation open to me. Were there others, tiny camps of people in the world who had survived, just like us? Were they kept in the dark too, about our history, or did they know about the day the sky froze?

Could I find my family?

Rainbows danced and glistened above me, begging for freedom. My palms itched. I curled my fingers, pressing against dampness pooling in the centre of my palm. A tiny, perfect, orb sat in the centre of my hand, balanced and unbreaking. I slipped my hand away, letting the drop float in the air before me. Through it, the hillside was inverted, grass above, sky below.

It dropped slowly, pressing into the ground, shattering outward. The earth sucked it up greedily.

The ground tremored, a tiny thing beneath my feet. Had She been waiting, all this time, for rain? Could it be that She hadn't trapped us, that we had trapped ourselves? A whisper of breeze flickered over me.

Jase followed me outside, yelling, but I blocked him out. He'd had his say. I loved him—there was no doubt. But I was *tired* of people telling me what to do, what not to do.

I breathed.

My arms prickled, went damp. I stretched them wide, encompassing all that I could. Above me, the sky moved, rippling like molten glass. The air closed in around me, stilled.

Above me, colours shifted. Ground and heavens melded; purple haze became a swirling maelstrom, flingers stretching to Earth, reaching.

Devouring.

In the palm of my hand, a drop formed, perfect and round, lifting from my skin, hovering. Floating.

A perfect orb of rain, rising.

# ACKNOWLEDGEMENTS

Wow, we got there! What began as a fun project took on a life of its own! There are so very many people who have helped bring Vertias to life, and every one of you are champions, thankyou!

To the amazing RH community for keeping me going every day with chats, memes and general mayhem, you guys are just incredible. Bo, Maya, Serena, Jodie, Jill, Dani...I could keep going with the names but just WOW. And thankyou!

To the Aussie authors who banded together when Vertias was on pre-order – I was blonw away by the local support. It's a huge thing to know you have your country's authors in your corner.

To my most patient and incredible husband, and my three crazy kids. You guys make it all worthwhile; the hours of stressing over plot holes and discussing the logistics of magic systems versus hard science over long distance phone calls at random hours. And that you think it's a good idea to keep wirting...well, ok!

My local writing groups, betas and ARC teams –

thank you so very, very much for all your efforts. Veritas is so much better for your eyes and attention!

To my amazing editor, Ashely – thankyou for working through lists of actions and descriptions on a stupidly short time frame – I promise we'll make the next one longer! Cheers for helping me through all the last minute freak outs!

To my most wonderful keyboard warriors, Jem and Jacinta. Vertias woulnd't exist without you. Thankyou for coffee nights where I planned a novel in a few sips and got stunned looks when I spluttered out something that made absolutely no sense at all – and yet, thanks to you, here she is, the Girl Who Brings the Rain. She is as much your baby as mine.

If you're a writer, or would like to be one day, please do something for me right now: go get a pen and some paper or open your laptop and *write*. And when you're finished, tell me. I want to read it, and I want to see a picture of you holding your book baby.

And to you, the reader, who made it all the way

through, following Jase, Veritas and Nestor. They will return, but first, we're taking a trip back in history, to meet their parents and find out what really happened in the Library.

Thankyou

Jo xxx

# About the Author

Jo Seysener is a mum of three crazy kids, a 32kg lounge shark who thinks she's a teacup puppy, and wife to the most amazing man and veteran. She writes picture books for Library For All, and speculative fiction for YA and adults. Jo would love to see you in her social media groups, and wants to make tea towels out of her reviews.

She adores alpacas.

www.joseysener.com

Jo's Gems - Jo Seysener Author public group | Facebook

www.facebook.com/joseysener

www.instagram.com/fancynancyer

www.twitter.com/JSeysener

#romancechallenge2020